THE
DUCK STREET GANG
RETURNS

Even ordinary school events – like a painting
competition – can quickly assume nightmare
proportions when Class 2D are around, so it's
no surprise that the headmaster of Duck
Street is just a little anxious when a TV company wish to use the infamous school for a
children's programme . . .

DENIS MARRAY

The
Duck Street Gang
Returns

A Magnet Book

For Mrs Jones

First published in 1986
by Hamish Hamilton Children's Books
This Magnet edition first published in 1987
by Methuen Children's Books Ltd
11 New Fetter Lane, London EC4P 4EE
Copyright © 1986 Denis Marray
Printed in Great Britain by
Richard Clay Ltd, Bungay, Suffolk

ISBN 0 416 04562 6

1

The early morning sun shone from a cloudless sky, warming the weather beaten bricks of Duck Street school. It also warmed the sturdy figure of Mr Croft, the school caretaker, who stood awhile enjoying the last moments of peace and quiet before opening the school gates for the first day of the new term.

The summer holidays had been a paradise of peace and quiet for Mr Croft. Sparrows had organised communal dust baths on the bare patches of ground, and little blades of grass protruded from between the flagstones. But now it was over. Mr Croft sighed heavily and consulted his pocketwatch. He decided that after opening the gates, he would make for the teachers' room, scrounge a cup of tea and add his gloom to the supply being generated by the teachers.

The thought appealed to him so much he almost cheered up, but he caught himself in time. Beside the main gate, the council had replaced the old battered sign with a new one on metal posts. It proclaimed that this was "Saint Balarics Comprehensive School", but only a few people in remote offices of the education committee called it Saint Balarics.

Everyone else called it Duck Street after the old

Victorian school it had replaced. As Mr Croft bolted the gates back, Mr Seymour, 2D's teacher, drove in, closely followed by Mr Dickens, the woodwork master. The depressed expressions on their faces as they nodded to him sent Mr Croft hurrying towards the staffroom.

Half an hour later he was sitting comfortably and enjoying a cup of tea as he listened to the teachers tell each other how quickly the past six weeks had flown. During a pause in the conversation, Mr Croft decided to contribute an anecdote of his own. He put down his cup and cleared his throat. The teachers looked at him expectantly.

"A couple of nights ago," he opened, "I was having a last look around the school, when I heard an owl."

"What was howling?" Mr Gamboge, the art master, asked.

"Nothing was howling," Mr Croft snapped.

"You said you heard a howl," Mr Gamboge persisted.

"No, I never," Mr Croft said shortly.

"Yes, you did," Mr Thomas, the sportsmaster, butted in. "I saw your lips moving."

Mr Croft gazed at the teachers with mounting irritation and they stared back straightfaced. With the exception of Mr Gamboge, who was inclined to be vague, they all knew what he meant.

"Not a *howl*," the caretaker explained, moving his lips slowly. "An owl." He stood and held his arms rigidly down his sides, then flapped them rapidly to indicate wings. "This kind of owl," he explained, turning his head slowly from left to right and calling out, "To-wit, to-woo."

At the end of the traverse, he found himself gazing at Mr Belham, the headmaster, who had just entered the room. There was a moment's silence, broken by a muffled giggle from Miss Lomax, the English teacher. "I was doing an owl," Mr Croft explained, giving his arms another little flap as an illustration.

"Very good," Mr Belham said without conviction. "And I hate to interrupt, but one of the kitchen staff has complained of a blocked sink. Would you attend to it?"

The caretaker nodded, his recently vanished gloom returning as he left the staffroom.

Considerably cheered, the teachers turned their attention to the headmaster. Mr Belham welcomed them back, and said he was sure they were refreshed by the holidays and raring to start the new term. Had he studied the expressions on their faces, he would have realised he was wrong on both counts, but he was busy with the clipboard that seemed part of his person.

"Here are the new class schedules for the Autumn term," he announced. "Pin them to the notice board and you can each make your own copy." He tucked the clipboard under his arm and glanced at his watch before bustling out of the room.

Someone pinned the schedules to the notice board and the teachers clustered around it apathetically until the first assembly bell of the new term sounded.

2D entered the classroom muttering "school" to each

other and shaking their heads in disbelief at the speed at which the holidays had passed. There was none of the usual pushing and shoving. The whole class moved like sleepwalkers.

Mr Seymour mounted the teachers' platform, put his books on the desk, and said, "Good morning 2D."

They replied, "Good morning, sir," without any great enthusiasm.

Mr Seymour pretended not to notice and called out the register. When he had finished he came around to the front of his desk and perched on the edge, looking down at a sea of depressed faces.

"I would like to remind you," he said, "that all of you will leave this school at some time. I, on the other hand, will be here until I retire."

2D stirred, murmured in horror and then fell to gazing at him compassionately.

Nellie Allbright, a big homely girl, was moved to comment. "There's always someone worse off than yourself, sir."

"A profound observation, Nellie," Mr Seymour said. "And I thank you for it."

"You're very welcome, sir," Nellie blushed.

Mr Seymour let his gaze wander over the healthy faces before him, and paused when he reached a bullet-headed, red-haired boy, Nathaniel Johnstone, known to all as Johnno.

"Johnstone," he asked. "Why is your skin hanging in shreds?"

"Sunburn, sir," Johnno replied. "I fell asleep on the shore and I nearly roasted myself alive. You can't be too careful if you have red hair. You should have seen me last week." He shook his head at his own stupidity. "I wasted a week of the holidays."

"A heartbreaking story," Mr Seymour said sympathetically.

"Just lying there in agony," Johnno brooded. "All my mates were away on holiday. The Ant was the only one to visit me."

Mr Seymour looked over at the Ant. Anthony Hopkins, the smallest boy in the class.

"Well done, Hopkins," he said. "To visit the sick is a cardinal act of mercy."

"No kidding, sir?" the Ant exclaimed. "I gave him a book an auntie had given me. Is that something else?"

"It comes under the same act," Mr Seymour explained.

"Then when he left," Johnno went on bitterly, "he told all the kids in the street I had leprosy. When I was well enough to go out, no one would come near me."

"That was cruel, Hopkins," Mr Seymour remarked, trying not to laugh with the rest of the class.

"I hate myself sometimes, sir," Ant sniggered.

Johnno leaned forward in his desk. "Did you know, sir, that the duck-billed platypus has a poisonous hook in its tail?"

"No, I didn't," Mr Seymour confessed.

"There's not many people do," Johnno said.

"I can believe that," Mr Seymour nodded.

"That was in the book of strange facts Ant gave me," Johnno beamed. "I can remember lots more interesting things. Do you want to hear them, sir?"

"Another time," Mr Seymour pleaded. "I'd like to muse on the platypus and its poisonous hook for a while."

"All right, sir," Johnno conceded. "Just give me the nod when you're ready."

Mr Seymour addressed 2D. "Did everyone else enjoy their holidays?" Ant interrupted a general murmur of assent. "I had a bad patch, sir," he said. "We were supposed to have a fortnight at a caravan camp, but we only had a week. It was my auntie's fault really. It wouldn't have happened if she hadn't cleared her attic out."

Mr Seymour held up his hand to stop the Ant. "Your aunt cleared the attic out and it ruined your holiday. Have I got that right?"

"Yes, sir," the Ant agreed. "She came across some books and she gave them to me. I took a couple to the caravan site with me in case it rained. One was about hunting and trapping. It showed you how to make a trap by bending a thin tree over and fixing a snare on it so that anything that gets caught is pulled into the air."

"Did you catch anything?" Mr Seymour asked.

"I didn't catch any animals," Ant admitted. "The man from the caravan next to us got caught in it. He was out jogging and he made a terrible fuss. I don't know why, it was only a small tree, and anyway, hopping on one leg is good exercise."

"Especially if you want one leg bigger than the other," Mr Seymour observed. "Do go on."

"The other book was called *A Thousand and One*

Things a Boy can Make. I made a kite," Ant brooded. "It took me all day and when I tried it out, it caught on a wire going across the camp, so I gave it a tug and there was a bang and a flash and everyone's telly went off." He brooded again. "Books can be dangerous," he concluded.

"You would be surprised," Mr Seymour said, "how many quite well known people have thought that."

He turned from the Ant and spoke to the class. "While your holidays are fresh in your mind, for your homework, I'd like you all to write an essay on the day you enjoyed most."

Big Davo, the tallest lad in the class, put his hand up. "The day I enjoyed the most, sir, was when I went sea-fishing in a boat. I caught a lot of mackerel, then came home. What is there to write about?"

"Re-live the day," Mr Seymour urged. "The smell and movement of the boat. How you felt when you caught the fish. Use your imagination."

"Brain's good at writing," Nellie Allbright said. "His is always the best."

"All right," Mr Seymour said amiably. He looked at the dark-haired lad sitting next to Johnno. Bartholomew Webster, alias "Brain".

"Webster," he said. "You are excused homework."

Brain smiled happily.

"I'll pick two winners," Mr Seymour sent on. "A boy and a girl, and they'll be excused homework for a week."

"I should be excused homework for a week because

I'm not going in for the competition, sir," Brain said hopefully.

"Don't push your luck, Webster," Mr Seymour advised.

When the lesson ended, Mr Seymour dismissed 2D and noticed that the inertia of the first day was already wearing off. Reflecting upon the resilience of youth, he made his way to the staffroom and found it in a state of uproar. Teachers clustered around Mr Belham's new class schedules talking excitedly to each other. Mr Seymour stood and watched for a while, then Mr Thomas signalled him from across the room, and he made his way over. The sportsmaster poured him a cup of tea. "What's all the excitement about?"

"The class schedules," Miss Lomax laughed. "They are all mixed up. Do you know I'm down to referee a football match this afternoon?"

Mr Seymour dropped a spoon into his cup and ambled over to his chair. The teachers all clustered about him.

"Do you know," said Mr Gamboge, "I'm down to take a woodwork class?"

"Do you know," Mr Dickens the woodwork teacher chipped in, "I'm down to take the girls at netball?"

"Do you know," Mr Seymour interrupted, "that the duck-billed platypus has a poisonous hook in its tail?"

The teachers glanced at each other and went quiet.

"No," Mr Thomas ventured after a moment. "We didn't know that."

Mr Seymour stirred his tea thoughtfully. "There's not many people do."

2

After he had called the register, Mr Seymour had Nellie Allbright collect the homework books and put them on his desk.

"I'm taking you for the last class of the day," Mr Seymour said, tapping the pile of homework books. "I'll have read your essays by then, and I'll let you know the winners of our little competition."

"I'll be one of the winners, sir," the Ant predicted. "Mine's brilliant." Mr Seymour banged his desk to stop the jeering. The Ant glared around the class. "I liked it so much I kept reading it," he said proudly. "You'll see."

"Hopkins," Mr Seymour pleaded. "You must try and fight that streak of modesty."

"I will, sir," the Ant promised.

"Excellent," Mr Seymour said. "Now let us proceed with the first mathematics lesson of the term."

Big Davo moaned softly.

"Are you in pain, Davis?" Mr Seymour enquired.

"I hate sums, sir," Big Davo explained. "They're boring."

"If you ever go sea-fishing, Davis, and find yourself

out of sight of land, I hope there is someone with you who found sums interesting."

2D considered this remark, then the Ant put his hand up. "My dad's uncle was a navigator in the Air Force, sir, he knew a lot about sums. He was in a bomber squadron, his plane was famous."

"What for?" Mr Seymour asked, interested.

"They bombed Glasgow twice, sir," Brain interrupted.

"They did not," the Ant shouted over the laughter.

"It may have been Edinburgh, sir," Brain admitted.

The Ant, who was fearless in one of his rages, prepared to hurl himself at Brain, and those in the vicinity tensed to move out of the way.

"Stop," Mr Seymour snapped, in a voice he seldom used.

Everyone froze, and even the Ant sat down meekly again.

Mr Seymour leaned on his desk looking at them, and 2D stared back uneasily.

When he spoke again, it was in his normal voice and the class gave a communal gasp of relief.

"I've never had a class like this one," he said. "No wonder my hair is going grey."

"It looks very distinguished, sir," Nellie Allbright soothed.

"Thank you, Nellie," Mr Seymour acknowledged. Then he turned to his desk and bent over a book trying to hide a smile.

Big Davo was still brooding on the horrors of mathematics.

"They're all barmy in sum books, sir," he said. "Trying to fill tanks with water at so many gallons a minute and the tanks leaking at so many pints a minute. No one in their right minds would try to fill a tank that was leaking."

"The problem is interesting mathematically," Mr Seymour protested.

"True, sir," Brain interrupted. "But psychologically depressing."

"You have a point," Mr Seymour admitted.

2D gazed proudly at Brain and Big Davo. They could grasp Big Davo's point, but were a little hazy about Brain's observation. Nevertheless they knew they were being championed and were ready to back them both.

Mr Seymour rubbed his chin thoughtfully. "I'll tell you what, 2D," he said. "I'll try and come up with an interesting problem every maths lesson, if you will try and tolerate demented plumbers and their ilk."

"You've got yourself a deal, sir," Johnno shouted over the general hubbub of agreement.

Mr Seymour went to the blackboard. "Interesting problem number one," he announced. He drew a wavy line. "That is the water level in a harbour. In this harbour there is a ship and over the side is a rope ladder with two rungs underwater. The rungs are eighteen inches apart. The tide rises nine inches every twenty minutes." He drew a quick sketch. "How many rungs will be under water in four hours?"

He dusted the chalk off his hands. "Write the problem down in your exercise books, and I want to see how you worked it out." He glanced at his watch. "You have ten minutes."

2D crouched over their books and silence fell upon the class. Mr Seymour sat at his desk and with a final glance at 2D, bent intently over their work, reached for a homework book and became absorbed.

The murmuring of voices broke his concentration, and he looked up at the class. "Everyone finished?" he asked.

There was a happy buzz of agreement.

"Judging from the muttering that went on," Mr Seymour continued, "I take it there has been some consultation about the answer?"

"Yes, sir," Johnno said proudly. "And we've all got it right."

Mr Seymour looked at Brain. "Everybody?"

"Yes, sir," Brain admitted thoughtfully.

"In that case," Mr Seymour said. "Let's have the answer."

Big Davo stood up. "Every forty minutes the tide rises one rung."

"That's six in four hours, sir," Nellie Allbright broke in.

"And two that were already in the water, sir," Joan Alison, a pretty, dark-haired girl, added.

"That makes eight," Nellie nodded, gazing at her friend proudly.

The class looked at Mr Seymour.

"Well, sir," Big Davo prompted. "Did we get it right?"

"I'm afraid not," said Mr Seymour.

2D gazed at him, stunned. Then pens were grabbed and further calculations made.

"It's eight rungs, sir," Big Davo sighed, and the class nodded agreement.

Mr Seymour grinned at them. "Let us leave that problem alone for a moment and visualise another ship in a harbour. Now the deck of this ship is ten feet higher than the water. If the water rises at two feet an hour, how long will it take to flood onto the deck and sink the ship?"

"It won't happen, sir," Big Davo protested. "The ship will always float on top of the water."

"Precisely," Mr Seymour nodded.

There was a moment's puzzled silence, then Brain threw his pen down in disgust. "*Two* rungs, sir, and I could kick myself."

Mr Seymour beamed at him. "Correct, Webster." He took in Brain's disgruntled expression and added, "Lo, the mighty are humbled."

"You're gloating, sir," Brain accused.

"You're right, Webster." Mr Seymour was affable. He sat on the edge of his desk and waited while the quicker-witted members of the class explained the answer to their classmates. Then the hubbub died down and 2D fell to gazing at Mr Seymour reproachfully.

"That's a trick sum, sir," Big Davo said.

Mr Seymour shook his head. "Everyone in this class knows that a ship floats. Where's the trick?"

"Well, we never thought about that bit, sir," Nellie Allbright sighed.

"That is the purpose of mathematics, Nellie," Mr Seymour explained. "It makes you think." He wiped the blackboard and began to write. "We shall now enter the world of a bunch of amiable lunatics, who are digging a trench at different speeds with shovels of different sizes. Copy the question in your exercise books, and then see if you can solve the problem."

2D's next lesson was art, and the classroom looked bare. All the best paintings and sketches from different classes that had been pinned around the wall, had gone, claimed by their proud owners and taken at the end of the old term. The barren walls reminded the class of the holidays recently ended, and the term stretching ahead. This had a somewhat depressing effect on 2D, and they settled down at their desks in half their usual time.

Mr Gamboge was rummaging in a large folder, and the absence of noise distracted him.

"Good morning, 2D," he said, peering down at them. "It is 2D?" He studied faces and nodded. "Welcome back."

He returned to the folder and after a while, sorted out a number of paintings and placed them on his desk. He then opened his briefcase and produced a newspaper, riffling through it briskly at first, then as some item caught his eye, he sank slowly into his chair and began to read it.

2D watched him gloomily for a while, then Big

Davo cleared his throat. Mr Gamboge looked up, startled. "Good morning, 2D."

"We've done that bit, sir," Johnno said.

"Ah, yes," Mr Gamboge nodded vaguely. He stood and leaned on his table. "Tell me, Johnstone, how would you like a bicycle or fishing rod or binoculars?"

"What would I have to do, sir?" Johnno countered cautiously.

Mr Gamboge picked up the paper. "Simply win a prize in a painting competition. It's being run by the local paper."

"I can't paint, sir," Johnno protested.

"You under-estimate yourself," Mr Gamboge said. He riffled through the paintings on his table. "This is a horse jumping. You did it before the holidays. While anatomically poor, it does convey a sense of movement." He showed the sketch to Johnno.

"That's supposed to be a frog, sir," Johnno said coldly, and 2D's gloom evaporated.

Mr Gamboge re-examined it. "It's got hooves," he objected.

"I hadn't finished its feet when the lesson ended, sir," Johnno explained.

"There's no problem, sir," Nellie Allbright grinned. "Ask him to paint a horse, it might look like a frog."

"Who asked you?" Johnno enquired.

"No one," Nellie was unabashed. "I was just trying to help you."

"Do me a favour," Johnno snarled. "Help somebody else. I'll bet I can paint a horse as good as anyone in this class."

"I don't particularly want anyone to paint a horse," Mr Gamboge protested. "I just wanted to point out that your painting, Johnstone, had a good sense of movement. Frog or horse, it doesn't matter. It looked as though it was jumping. Do you understand?"

Johnno scratched his head. "I think so, sir. Do all the paintings go into this competition?"

"Yes," said Mr Gamboge. He brandished the paper. "They're not looking for masterpieces, so don't despair."

"When is the closing date?" Brain asked.

Mr Gamboge hesitated. "Now there we have a problem. I don't normally get this paper, the competition was pointed out to me by one of the other teachers this morning. To enter the competition, I'm afraid you must complete the painting by the end of this lesson."

2D moaned in despair.

"We've no chance," Big Davo mourned.

Nellie Allbright jumped to her feet. "Then we'd best get started. Me and Joan will hand out the paper and paints, sir."

"Well done, Nellie," Mr Gamboge encouraged. "That's the spirit."

"We've absolutely no chance," Big Davo reiterated.

Nellie started handing out the papers, and Joan Alison passed round the paints. "You never know what you can do until you try," Nellie said briskly. "Are we going to have a go, or are we going to quit before we start?" Nellie was at her best in a crisis, and 2D responded.

"Put the title and your name and age on the bottom," Mr Gamboge called.

Within minutes, the whole class was staring at blank sheets of paper with great ferocity.

The Ant was first to make a move. "I've got a feeling I'm going to win this competition," he announced.

2D were too absorbed to react to the claim.

Nellie Allbright had been to two weddings during the holidays, and was somewhat obsessed with the subject. Tongue protruding, she carefully painted in the arched doorway where her bride and groom would stand.

Big Davo made a tentative start on a clipper ship, which he hoped would resemble the picture that hung in the local library.

Time flew, and the class jumped with surprise when Mr Gamboge glanced at his watch and called, "Five more minutes."

Nellie decided a little more red on the bridesmaid's dress would add the finishing touch. She put a little too much colour on the brush and to her horror, saw a large blob forming on the end. She gave the brush a quick flick over her shoulder and examined it again. Behind her the Ant gazed in disbelief at the big red blots that had appeared on his painting. He raised his eyes and glared at the back of Nellie's head.

Nellie decided that there was still a little too much paint on the brush and gave it another shake. Small red dots appeared on the Ant's face, which immediately purpled with rage. He tapped Nellie on the shoulder. "Look what you did to my face," he snarled.

Nellie and Joan Alison looked at his spotty face and started giggling.

The Ant coated his brush with black paint and pushing Nellie aside, made five black vertical slashes down the length of her painting. Nellie and her hench-woman, Joan Alison, gasped in horror, gazing first at the painting, then at each other.

Nellie's face became grim, and with a hand that shook with rage, she wet her brush and rubbed it fiercely across the paints. Divining her friend's intention, Joan did the same. Then they both turned. Before the Ant could stop them they whirled a kaleidoscope of colour over his painting.

2D stopped what they were doing and gathered silently around. They watched the Ant coat his brush with black paint and lunge again at Nellie's picture. They nodded approval at the way Nellie blocked the movement and held him, then chuckled when Joan snatched the brush from his hand and painted a thick straight moustache across his face.

Then the bell went for the end of the lesson and at the same time the headmaster strode in.

"Clean your brushes and put your paints neatly on your desks," Mr Gamboge ordered, turning to the headmaster. 2D did as they were told, and the Ant kept Big Davo between the headmaster and himself as they left the classroom. The rest of 2D turned left in the corridor and made for the playground, but the Ant spun right and strode down the corridor towards the wash-rooms, muttering to himself.

Mr Thomas stepped out of a classroom and the Ant crashed into his legs. "Steady on," the burly sports-master said mildly.

"Sorry, sir." The Ant picked himself up and strode on.

Mr Thomas, who had caught a glimpse of the Ant's face, made for the teachers' room and a welcome break.

In the main corridor he met Mr Seymour ambling along to the same destination.

Mr Seymour gazed at his colleague. "What's wrong?" he asked.

"Did you take 2D for the first lesson this morning?" the sportsmaster enquired.

Mr Seymour nodded.

"Was Hopkins healthy and clean shaven?" Mr Thomas persisted.

Mr Seymour gave another bewildered nod.

"Well," Mr Thomas continued, "since you saw him last, he appears to have grown a moustache and contracted measles."

2D straggled into Mr Seymour's class for the last lesson of the day

"I'd have won that painting competition if it hadn't been for Nellie Allbright," the Ant complained to Johnno and Brain. "It was a smashing painting."

"We saw it," Brain said. "And I just can't see a painting of a fried egg winning the competition."

"It was a sunset," the Ant snapped.

"In that case," Johnno interrupted, "it definitely had no chance."

Mr Seymour rapped on his desk and the murmur of voices died down. "Before we begin our lesson," Mr Seymour began. "I'll tell you the results of our little essay competition."

The Ant put up his hand. "I won, didn't I, sir?"

"No, you didn't," Mr Seymour contradicted. "I asked for an essay on a day of your holidays. One day, Hopkins. You covered the whole holidays, and it reads like a report from one of Attila the Hun's more able lieutenants."

The Ant scowled ferociously, and folded his arms with the air of someone who has wiped his hands of the whole affair.

"To continue," Mr Seymour went on, ignoring the Ant's glare, "I was pleasantly surprised at the quality of the essays. Do try and keep up this standard. Now the winner for the girls is Joan Alison. Well done, Joan."

Nellie Allbright beamed at her blushing henchwoman.

"And the winner amongst the boys is one David Davis."

Big Davo's jaw dropped. "Me, sir?"

"You, sir," Mr Seymour confirmed.

Big Davo shook his head. "I've never done anything like that before, sir."

"There's a first time for everything, Davis," Mr Seymour said. "No homework for a week. Keep it up!" He turned to the blackboard and began to write. "This lesson will be a quick recap on the history lessons you had last term. It will refresh your memories. We'll start with the kings and queens of England, how long they reigned and where they are buried."

When he turned to face the class again, Johnno had his hand up. Mr Seymour threw the chalk onto his desk. "Yes, Johnstone?"

"Talking about burying people, sir," Johnno said proudly. "Did you know that Chief Black Bird of the Omaha Indians was buried sitting on his horse?"

The teacher stared at Johnno in amazement. "On his horse, Johnstone?"

"Yes, sir," Johnno confirmed.

"Didn't you know that, sir?" Brain grinned.

"No," Mr Seymour confessed. "The subject never came up when I was at teachers' training college. In retrospect, I can't think why. Where did you get your information from, Johnstone?"

"The book the Ant gave me, sir," Johnno said proudly. "Remember the duck-billed platypus?"

"Ah," said Mr Seymour. "The duck-billed platypus. *That* book."

"It must have been a hell of a deep hole, sir. It must have taken ages to dig it." Big Davo said, fascinated by Johnno's latest amazing fact.

"The whole tribe probably got busy," Johnno hazarded. "Hundreds of them."

Nellie Allbright jumped to her feet, the animal lover in her outraged. "Was the horse dead?" she asked.

"It is now," Big Davo sniggered.

Nellie glared at him, then appealed to Mr Seymour.

"This sort of thing wants stopping, sir."

"I agree, Miss Allbright," Mr Seymour said. "Although I don't imagine it happens very often."

"They probably killed it after he died, sir," Nellie said brokenly. "It's not fair."

Mr Seymour closed his eyes and took a deep breath. "It happened a very long time ago. There's nothing we can do."

"There must be something, sir," Nellie pleaded.

"Well, you could picket the local undertaker's until they promise not to bury people sitting on horses," Mr Seymour said wearily.

The class began to argue noisily. Mr Seymour slammed both his hands on the desk and roared, "Enough."

2D fell still. Groups that were arguing for and against the time of the horse's demise subsided.

Mr Seymour let the silence stay unbroken for a while, then he said, "Anyone fascinated by the burial customs of the North American Indian, and the problems involved, can consult Johnstone after school hours. Now open your exercise books and copy what is on the blackboard."

The class bent over their books and began to write. Mr Seymour sat at his desk and watched them alertly at first, then the gentle mumbling noise of 2D copying from the blackboard soothed him and he began to relax.

Lacing his hands behind his head, he found himself visualising a tribe of Indians carrying a horse and rider, staggering towards a huge hole.

3

Mr Seymour sat and gazed absently at the part of Duck Street school that could be seen from the driver's seat. The last straggling pupils had left and his was the only car in the school car park.

The afternoon sun glinted on the large area of windows and weather-beaten rustic brick. He wondered, and not for the first time, if the powers that be, who had named the school Saint Balarics, had thought the local inhabitants would call it that.

If they had, it was a gross error of judgement. If the government were to pull down Buckingham Palace and re-erect it on the site, it would be known locally as Duck Street palace.

He glanced at his watch and hoped that Mr Croft, the school caretaker, would not be long.

With the help of Mr Dickens, Mr Seymour had built a large greenhouse in his garden and Mr Croft, overhearing them talking about it, had told him that a friend of his was a park keeper, and he had an oil heater to sell at a reasonable price. He would also throw in some winter chrysanthemums as a gesture of goodwill.

He was about to glance at his watch again, when he saw Mr Croft hurrying towards him.

"Sorry I'm late," the caretaker said, scrambling in beside him and slamming the car door shut.

Mr Seymour started the engine and moved across the car park. Mr Croft fumbled with his seat belt. "I've been arguing with the cleaning ladies," he said. He fastened the belt and brooded quietly until they neared Yardley Park.

"Head for the parkie's house on the corner," he instructed. "The gate will be open."

Mr Seymour turned into the driveway of a large, early-Victorian house and stopped the car.

They both got out and gazed around. On the other side of a neatly clipped hedge were rows of council owned hothouses, and beyond them, the bowling greens.

There was no sign of the park keeper.

"He said he would be around the house at this time," Mr Croft fretted. "He might be in his own garden at the back."

As they walked around the gable end of the house, they could hear a hoarse voice shouting angrily.

Mr Croft cupped a hand to his ear. "That sounds like him."

At the far end of the back garden stood a huge horse-chestnut tree, and facing it was a bearded burly man in a park keeper's uniform. They watched as he struck the tree a couple of angry blows with a stick and shouted again.

"He certainly keeps a well disciplined park," Mr Seymour said.

Mr Croft strode ahead calling, "Charlie, we're here about the stove."

The park keeper turned from the tree as they approached.

"Worse than Dutch elm disease," he snapped.

"What is, Charlie?" Mr Croft enquired. The park keeper raised his stick and pointed into the tree. "That," he grunted.

Mr Seymour gazed up at the foliage, and after a couple of seconds made out a face staring down at him. His heart sank. "Get down out of that tree, Hopkins," he ordered. Then to the park keeper, "Will you let me handle this?"

"Gladly," the park keeper nodded. "Come on, Albert," he said to Mr Croft. "You can give me a hand to carry the stove around to the front."

When they had left the vicinity of the tree, the Ant began a cautious descent.

"You will write 'I must not trespass' one hundred times, Hopkins," Mr Seymour ordered.

"I was looking for conkers, sir," pleaded the Ant.

"In that case, Hopkins, write 'I must not trespass in search of conkers' one hundred times," Mr Seymour said pleasantly.

"I don't think I can spell trespass, sir." The Ant was mournful.

"It's of no consequence," Mr Seymour assured him. "As I am the only person in the British Isles who can decipher your handwriting, your spelling shall be a secret between us."

He looked around the garden. "How did you get in here?"

"Through a gap in the hedge in the far end, sir," the Ant said.

"Then kindly exit the same way."

"Yes, sir," the Ant wandered off, dejected.

Mr Seymour shook his head and joined Mr Croft and the park keeper at the front of the house.

They had the heater by the car, ready to put it in the boot. As Mr Seymour approached, the park keeper tapped it with his foot.

"It's a good 'un," he said. "But it needs cleaning."

"I'll take it," Mr Seymour said.

"You'll not regret it," the park keeper beamed. "I've got your chrysanths just inside the door, I'll go and get them."

After dropping the caretaker off at the school, Mr Seymour drove home and unloaded his chrysan-themums, then he took the heater out of the boot and studied it for a few moments before deciding not to clean it right away. He pushed it under the garage workbench out of the way and went into the house, smelling slightly of paraffin.

As he entered, his wife was setting the table.

"Hello, love," he said. "I've got the heater, but it needs cleaning."

His wife wrinkled her nostrils. "So do you."

"Give me five minutes," Mr Seymour grinned, heading for the bathroom.

"Don't forget it's the social club this evening," his wife called after him.

The social club was almost empty when they

arrived. The members were sitting in the spacious grounds at the back, drinking tea and chatting, enjoying the late afternoon sun. Mrs Seymour moved a few paces away from her husband to speak to some friends. Mr Seymour looked around as he waited. It was a pleasant scene, the small tables set around the edge of the bowling green, the clink of tea cups and the murmur of voices. By sheer chance his eyes had reached a couple sitting under a horse-chestnut tree. The man was leaning over the table to light his companion's cigarette, when there was a crack like a pistol shot, and an object crashed down out of the tree and landed on him. Both man and table collapsed, and his companion jumped back screaming and fell over her chair.

In the moment's horrified pause that followed, the object that had fallen from the tree staggered into the shrubbery. People helped the couple to their feet, and the man stood trying to suck back into his lungs the air that had been driven out by the impact.

The table lay with one leg almost hanging off. His eye fell upon it, and, spending some of the hard won oxygen in a scream of rage, he tore it completely off and leapt into the shrubbery flailing about like a madman. Friends tried to soothe him, but he was like a man possessed.

A pace or two away from where Mr Seymour stood, a large shrub stirred uneasily.

Mr Seymour faced it.

"Hopkins," he said. "Make that two hundred lines."

The shrub moaned softly, and was still.

Mr Seymour turned and found his wife gazing at him with considerable curiosity.

"I've been coming here for years," she said. "And I never knew that hydrangea's name was Hopkins."

4

Mr Seymour ambled into the teachers' room the next morning and found Constable Dukinfield, helmet off, taking a tentative sip of a cup of tea.

Duck Street school was on his beat and he often dropped in to enlist the teachers' aid in imparting information, and the occasional warning, to the pupils.

Mr Seymour nodded to the constable and, dropping his briefcase by his chair, poured himself a cup of tea, and waited with the other teachers for the constable to make his announcement.

"It's the suspense I can't stand," Miss Lomax said to Mr Thomas.

Constable Dukinfield put his cup down and cleared his throat. Immediately the murmur of conversation ceased and all eyes were expectantly on him.

"As you may or may not know," he began, "the Boy Scouts in this area have started a 'plant a tree scheme'. Groups of them have been going around under supervision, planting the whizzers off sycamore trees and the conkers off horse-chestnuts. The owners of the horse-chestnut trees were glad to co-operate because they reasoned that this would prevent the annual attack by hordes of local children in search of conkers.

Unfortunately this has caused a certain amount of animosity between the local children and the Scouts. If you could explain to your pupils that they will benefit in the long run from there being more conker trees, it might help the situation."

The teachers considered Constable Dukinfield's request, and he looked around hopefully.

"We'll do our best," Mr Seymour nodded. "But as the pupils will be drawing their old age pension before the trees are big enough for a conker supply, I can't see them being impressed by your argument."

"There's a big horse-chestnut tree in the station yard," Constable Dukinfield went on gloomily. "One of our cars was parked under it. The other evening a small boy fell out of the tree, damaged the roof of the car and made good his escape. It's got to stop."

"The problem will solve itself," Mr Thomas put in. "The conker craze only lasts a week or two."

"They won't let it pass," Mr Seymour predicted. "All the schools in the area will be mounting expeditions to the countryside."

"I don't care what they do in the countryside," Constable Dunkinfield said selfishly, "as long as my patch stays quiet." He picked up his helmet, tucked it under his arm and bade them good morning.

There was a short silence following his exit, and in it Mr Gamboge got up from his chair and poured himself another cup of tea, shaking his head and sighing heavily.

"Is there anything wrong, Mr Gamboge?" Miss Lomax asked.

"I was thinking about dogs with no teeth," Mr

Gamboge said. He went back to his chair and began to sip his tea.

The teachers circled his chair and his friend, Mr Dickens, shook his shoulder. "You were speaking of toothless dogs," he prompted. "Do go on."

Mr Gamboge looked at him sadly. "I learned yesterday that dogs' teeth were used as money in the Solomon Islands eighty years ago, and I have been wondering since if they were taken from dead dogs or live ones." He looked at the teachers gathered around his chair. "You must think me odd."

"Of course not," Miss Lomax said stoutly.

"Insane, possibly," Mr Thomas sniggered, then grunted as Miss Lomax's elbow dug into his ribs.

At this moment Mr Croft came into the room. "Any chance of a quick cup – " he began. Then he saw the way the teachers were grouped around Mr Gamboge.

"Has he fainted?" he asked.

"No," Mr Thomas replied. "He's worried about dogs with no teeth."

"Where are they?" Mr Croft enquired, his interest aroused.

"They lived on the Solomon Islands eighty years ago," Mr Seymour said.

Mr Croft digested this information. "They'd be dead by now."

"Very likely," Mr Seymour nodded.

"Well, what's he worried about them for?" the caretaker asked.

Mr Seymour grasped his elbow gently. "Would you like a cup of tea?"

Mr Croft let himself be led away. "I'm parched," he admitted. The group around Mr Gamboge broke up, and Mr Croft accepted his tea and took a couple of noisy sips. "Funny thing, the human mind," he announced. "I had an uncle once who thought he was a hen."

"What sort of a hen?" Mr Thomas asked.

"I couldn't say," Mr Croft admitted. "I don't know much about hens. They had a big dog-basket and he'd sit in it for hours sometimes, clucking away."

"Your poor aunt must have been upset," Miss Lomax was sympathetic.

"She got used to him," Mr Croft assured her. "The dog didn't though. It used to get very annoyed. It took to sleeping on the sofa."

Mr Gamboge joined the group, gummy dogs forgotten.

"How did the situation resolve itself?" he asked.

"Eh?" said Mr Croft.

"What happened in the end?" Mr Seymour translated.

"Ah," Mr Croft nodded. "Well, one night my uncle and the dog headed for the basket, and my uncle got there first and the dog bit him. My uncle lost his temper. He said it was a bad sort of dog that would attack a hen, and either the dog went or he did. My auntie told him to leave it with her, and a couple of days later a van drew up outside the house and two blokes in white coats got out."

"They took the poor dog and had it put down?" Miss Lomax interrupted, her voice trembling.

"No," Mr Croft contradicted. "They took my uncle. The dog lived for years afterwards."

In the stunned silence that followed the story, Mr Thomas said, "You're pulling our legs."

"No, honest," Mr Croft said earnestly. He looked about the room and selected a corner by the door.

"Imagine this corner is a dog-basket," he said. He knelt down, put his fists on his chest and gave his elbows an experimental flap. Then he sat back on his heels, hunched his shoulders and began clucking.

At this point the headmaster bustled into the room, clip board and papers held in front of him. He saw Mr Croft and halted so abruptly he almost overbalanced.

The caretaker, head back and eyes shut, was in the middle of a violent bout of clucking.

Mr Belham looked wide-eyed at the teachers.

"He was telling us about his uncle," Mr Gamboge explained.

The headmaster swung his gaze back to Mr Croft, trying to equate his behaviour with an anecdote about his family.

"He thought he was a hen," Mr Gamboge enlarged.

"Mr Croft?"

"His uncle."

The caretaker lowered his head and the clucking stopped.

"Two men in white coats came and took his uncle away," Mr Gamboge went on.

"Really," said Mr Belham, staring fixedly at Mr Croft. Then the assembly bell rang and Mr Croft got to his feet and saw the headmaster.

"Good morning, Mr Belham," he said cheerfully. "I was telling them about my uncle."

"So I believe," Mr Belham acknowledged. "He was insane?"

"Lord, no." The caretaker was shocked. "He just thought he was a hen."

The headmaster vented a deep sigh and consulted his clipboard. "Miss Lomax and Mr Thomas, could you spare a moment? I want a word with you both concerning forthcoming team events."

Mr Seymour was strolling along the corridor towards his classroom when he heard hurried footsteps behind him. He turned and saw the Ant.

"Hopkins. You're just the lad I want to see."

"Yes, sir?" the Ant said cautiously.

"You do know that the Scouts have stripped every conker tree for miles around?"

"Yes, sir," the Ant said again.

"Then," Mr Seymour said patiently, "why do you persist in looking for them?"

"I thought they might have left a few higher up," the Ant explained. "I'm very good at climbing trees."

"Your ability at tree climbing is not being questioned, Hopkins," the teacher looked at him sternly. "However, your method of descending from trees is causing a lot of local comment. I want you to cease."

"You want me to stop?" the Ant probed.

"Precisely, Hopkins," Mr Seymour beamed.

"All right, sir," the Ant conceded. "It's a waste of time anyway."

"Good," Mr Seymour said. "Now, the next item on the agenda is your lines. Have you done them?"

"Yes, sir." The Ant fumbled in his satchel and handed Mr Seymour an exercise book.

The teacher studied it as they walked along the corridor. When they reached the classroom, Mr Seymour sighed and handed the Ant the exercise book.

"Are they all right, sir?" the Ant asked anxiously.

"Yes," said Mr Seymour. "They appear to be written in secret code, but as I didn't specify a language, I feel that I am to blame." He opened the classroom door and gestured inside. "After you."

When he had called the register, Mr Seymour quickly got the class working. He was aided by the weather which was very warm, making 2D a lot less active than usual. He walked between their desks as they bent over their books, then he noticed Nellie Allbright chewing her pen, and staring absently into the middle distance.

"Do you understand the question, Nellie?" he asked.

Nellie started in surprise. "Yes, sir," she said, bending over her book.

Mr Seymour looked at her thoughtfully, then went back to his desk and began correcting the class's homework. A few times he happened to look up and Nellie was staring ahead in a very preoccupied manner.

When the bell went for the end of the lesson, 2D livened up a little. As they were leaving the classroom, Mr Seymour called, "Nellie, can I see you for a moment." Nellie stopped at his desk and waited apathetically.

Mr Seymour carried on marking the homework books until the classroom was empty. Joan Alison was the last to leave, throwing a sympathetic glance at her friend before she went.

Mr Seymour put down his pen. "What's wrong, Nellie?" he asked gently.

"It's them octopuses, sir," she blurted, after a pause. "I can't get them out of my mind."

Mr Seymour's jaw dropped. "Octopuses, Nellie? You did say octopuses?"

"Yes, sir," Nellie confirmed. "They commit suicide by eating their own tentacles when in captivity. It shouldn't be allowed, sir."

Mr Seymour was stunned for a moment. First Mr Gamboge and his gummy dogs, now Nellie and octopuses.

"Who told you about the octopuses, Nellie?" Mr Seymour asked.

"Johnno, sir," she said. "From his book of strange facts."

"Ah," Mr Seymour murmured, as understanding dawned. Then he looked at Nellie's unhappy face. "It must be an old book, Nellie. They keep octopuses in captivity in most modern aquariums, so they must have solved the problem."

Nellie's face brightened. "Are you sure, sir?"

"Positive," Mr Seymour said firmly.

"Oh thank you, sir," Nellie was her old self again. "I was worried."

When she had left the classroom, Mr Seymour stuffed the homework books into his briefcase and made his way to the teachers' room a little more rapidly than usual.

Mr Thomas was standing holding a cup in a listless hand, watching a group of teachers clustered around a window. He saw Mr Seymour enter and came over to him.

"It's happening, boyo," the big Welshman said gloomily. "We're starting to crack up. It could be my turn next."

"Calm yourself," Mr Seymour pleaded, pouring a cup of tea.

Mr Thomas gestured to the group at the window. "Do you know what they are doing?"

Mr Seymour sugared and milked the tea. "Tell me."

Mr Thomas sat next to Mr Seymour and leaned forward. "They are trying to figure out how to get a gas mask on a pigeon."

Mr Seymour looked at him in amazement. "How did the subject arise?"

Mr Thomas hesitated. "I'm afraid it was Miss Lomax. She came in a few moments ago, saw the birds on the sill outside and asked us if we knew that the French had designed gas masks for pigeons in world war two."

"Johnstone is to blame," Mr Seymour said.

"No," Mr Thomas contradicted. "It was a Frenchman."

"I mean," Mr Seymour said patiently, "that he has

in his possession a book of oddities, and he is going around infecting everyone with bizarre facts."

Mr Thomas pondered the information. "How did you find out?"

"I should have realised earlier," Mr Seymour said. "Remember the duck-billed platypus? But it was Nellie Allbright who put me on to him. She was rather upset in class today. Apparently Johnstone told her that octopuses commit suicide by eating their tentacles when in captivity."

"Oh, how awful," a voice behind them moaned.

Both teachers turned and saw Mr Gamboge looking very distressed. He poured himself a coffee, tut-tutting and shaking his head. At this point the pigeons, embarrassed by being stared at, flew off with an indignant clatter of wings. The group at the window straightened and turned just as Mr Gamboge drifted past.

"The poor, poor creatures," he was muttering.

"Pigeons?" someone asked.

"No," he said brokenly. "Octopuses. What a terrible way to commit suicide."

Instead of breaking up, the group followed Mr Gamboge down the room.

5

It was a painting by Mr Gamboge that started it all.
Brain, Johnno and Big Davo had gone to the library to
change their books, and on exhibition were paintings
by local artists. Included were three paintings by Mr
Gamboge. This triggered off their interest, and they
examined the paintings minutely. Two were country
scenes, but the one that held their attention was of a
disused dock, bordered by a derelict warehouse.

Johnno and Big Davo fell to arguing about the
location of the dock, each convinced he knew where
it was. The argument became rather heated, and the
librarian came into the children's section and threatened
to eject them. When he had gone they continued the
argument in hoarse whispers, which proved so tiring on
the throat, they turned to Brain to act as an arbiter.

He was absorbed by the other two paintings,
especially the one depicting a large country house and
woods bordered by a high wall.

"Brain," Johnno pleaded. "Come here a minute."

"Look, lads," Brain said excitedly, ignoring his
request. "Do you see the painting of the big house? Now
look at the other painting of a village and church. Over

in the corner above the trees is the roof of the same big house."

Johnno and Big Davo examined the paintings without interest.

"Oh yeah," Johnno commented.

"Absolutely amazing." Big Davo was mildly sarcastic.

Brain tutted in exasperation. "Look at the trees all around the big house, they're horse-chestnuts."

Johnno and Big Davo examined the paintings with renewed interest.

"They've got white flower things on them," Johnno objected.

"They turn into conkers," Brain explained.

"No kidding?" Big Davo was impressed. "Isn't nature wonderful?"

"Now, all we've got to do is find out from Mr Gamboge where the village is, and if it's not too far we can bring home loads of conkers and sell what we don't need." Brain looked at his friends. "OK?"

"You're brilliant, mate," Johnno said respectfully.

By unspoken consent, Johnno and Big Davo let Brain plan the strategy. He waited patiently until the next art class, and when it was over he took his time putting things away and then, unobtrusively, helped Mr Gamboge.

The classroom emptied with its usual rapidity, Johnno and Big Davo casually took their time, making sure they were the last out of the room, leaving Brain a clear field.

It was possible they overdid the casualness, because

Nellie Allbright and Joan Alison glanced at them suspiciously, but said nothing.

The cause of their secrecy was not greediness. They realised that unless they kept quiet about their plan, word would spread along the grapevine. The possibility then existed that not only the rest of the class might join in, but other classes. Even classes from other schools. If such a horde descended upon the area, the forces of law and order would be alerted, and the result would be a shambles. On the other hand, a small well-planned commando raid had every chance of success.

When Brain joined the others in the playground, break was nearly over.

"Well?" Johnno asked.

"I've found the name of the village and church," Brain said. "The big house is owned by the council and they run Advanced Education courses there. That means there won't be any game-keepers in the woods. The village has a market every Saturday, so there are plenty of buses."

"Great," Big Davo said happily. "How do we get there?"

"Mr Gamboge reckons it's over twenty miles," Brain admitted.

"We can go down to the bus depot after school and find out what buses we have to get, and more important – "

"How much it is," Johnno finished. "That'll be a problem, I'm skint."

"So am I," Big Davo said gloomily.

"Me too," Brain admitted. "But it'll be the

weekend before we can go, so if we plan everything we'll be ready if we get the money."

Johnno and Big Davo nodded agreement.

"Who's in with us?" Big Davo asked.

Brain considered. "Nellie Allbright and Joan Alison for a start. They can climb as good as boys, and people don't seem to watch as close if there's girls with you."

"We'll ask them to make sandwiches to take with us. They make smashing sarnies," Johnno stated happily.

"We'll *all* bring sandwiches," Brain said sternly.

"'Course we will," Big Davo soothed. "But they seem to get eaten fast. It's all the fresh air, it makes you hungry."

Johnno had been pondering. "What about the Ant? He's good at climbing trees. He falls out of them now and again, but he doesn't care."

"That's because he always lands on his head," Big Davo sniggered. A thought struck him. "He always yells when he falls. That might give us away."

"We'll make him promise to fall quietly," Brain grinned. "That'll be the team, then. Six of us, and it'll have to be kept secret or we've no chance."

They wandered casually across the playground looking out for Nellie and Joan, or the Ant, turning down an invitation to a kick around with a tennis ball, and avoiding a group of friends swapping comics.

Big Davo spotted Nellie and Joan by the bike sheds. "They're on their own too," he reported happily.

* * *

"We're in," Nellie said, when the plan was explained to her, and Joan nodded agreement.

"The problem is, we don't have any money either. Mind you, we'll have our pocket money by the week-end. That should help."

Brain shook his head doubtfully. "It won't be enough. Perhaps the Ant could help out."

"I doubt it," Joan said. "He went fishing on Saturday and he borrowed twenty-five pence off Nellie and me for maggots and bus fare."

"That's torn it," Johnno murmured sadly.

"Speak of the devil," said Nellie. "Here he comes."

The group turned and saw the diminutive figure of the Ant swaggering towards them.

"'Lo lads," he nodded. "Hang on a minute." He fumbled in his pocket and produced two fifty-pence pieces. He gave Nellie one and Joan the other.

"Twenty-five pence I owe you girls each and the other twenty-five is for lending it to me."

"Ant," Brain asked hopefully. "Are you in the money?"

"Am I?" Ant bragged. "One of my uncles came home from Australia for a holiday, and he bunged me a tenner."

The group beamed at him and Johnno threw an arm around his shoulders.

The Ant glanced suspiciously from face to face. "You're after my money," he concluded.

"Ant," said Johnno, giving him a friendly squeeze. "How long have you been a mind reader?"

* * *

The following Saturday, the six left their homes early and met at a pre-arranged spot, laden with plastic carrier bags bulging with sandwiches and lemonade.

Brain surveyed them happily. "So far so good," he said. "No one late, that's a good omen."

"Have you all got plenty of spare bags to put the conkers in?" Big Davo asked.

"Oodles," the Ant replied. "Let's get going."

"He's talking sense," Nellie grunted, hefting her bag. "He must be sick."

They trailed trustfully after Brain and reached the bus station with ten minutes to spare. Brain quickly found the right bus and they clambered on board. The driver eyed their carrier bags.

"It's a nice day for a picnic," he said cheerfully, as he took their fares.

They agreed and scrambled onto the top deck, scuffling for the front seats.

"Right," said Brain, in the interval between getting settled and the bus moving off. "We'll go over the plan again. When we get to the woods, we get all the conkers we can carry. Then we get out again and get the next bus back. No exploring or messing about."

He looked at Nellie and Joan. "And no picking flowers or feeding ducks and things."

Everyone nodded happy agreement and they settled down as the bus started.

When the bus arrived at its destination, they had half an hour to wait for the next one and they spent it examining the nearby canal. Trees overhung the banks and the water was crystal clear.

"Is that the same canal that goes around our way?" Johnno asked.

"That's it," Brain confirmed, pointing to the Pennine Hills that could be seen in the distance. "It goes right over them to Leeds."

"It's *luvly*," Nellie sighed. "Let's sit here a minute and have a sangwidge."

The motion was quickly seconded and they made themselves comfortable on a patch of soft grass. As the sandwiches were produced, a family of ducks came out of a patch of reeds and paddled towards them, line astern.

Nellie and Joan gave cries of delight and threw them pieces of bread.

"I thought we weren't supposed to feed ducks and that?" Johnno asked.

"Only after we get the conkers," Big Davo explained.

The Ant, who had wandered further along the tow path eating a sandwich, suddenly pointed to the canal and shouted incoherently through a mouthful of bread.

The lads ran over to see what had excited him.

"Perch," the Ant spluttered, spraying them with breadcrumbs. "Dozens of them."

They clustered at the edge of the bank, and, shading their eyes, gazed into the water. A large shoal of perch swam lazily past.

"The size of them," Big Davo marvelled. "I wish we'd brought our rods."

"We're here to get conkers," Brain pointed out. He

broke off as he caught sight of the girls, jumping up and down and pointing. "Heck lads, the bus is in."

They charged down to where the girls were waiting, and grabbed at their gear, arriving breathless at the bus stop where a single-decker bus stood.

The bus driver was standing at the door chatting to the passengers as they climbed leisurely aboard.

They sat at the back of the bus and got their breath back as the bus began to move off. The route seemed to consist of narrow lanes, with the hedgerows scratching at the windows, then steep hills from where they could see for miles.

Then after all the stops and starts, the bus turned into a small village, and the hiss of its brakes when it stopped had an air of finality.

Brain said, "We're here."

6

The village square was crowded and they made their way to the shady side of the street, and put their bags down. There was a pleasant cooling breeze blowing and Nellie faced it. "That wind is luvly," she said. "It was like an oven on that bus."

Brain looked around. On the far side of the square was a war memorial that was in Mr Gamboge's paintings, and from this he took his bearings.

They followed him without question, and he led them out of the village and along a narrow country road. On their left they could see a large wood surrounded by a high wall.

Johnno halted. "Are they all conker trees?" he asked.

"Most of them," said Brain.

"There must be thousands," Big Davo said happily.

Joan Alison was gazing into the distance. "I don't want to worry you," she remarked. "But the road is turning away from the woods."

"There'll be a side road off this one," Brain predicted. "There's bound to be. The people in the big house had to get in and out."

The light breeze seemed to have died down, and

they marched along the deserted road, swiping irritably at flies and midges, for over a mile before they came upon the side road.

It was quite long, but at the end of it they could see huge iron gates. Unconsciously, they speeded up their walk, fatigue and flies forgotten, but as they neared the gates the silence was broken by the sound of a heavy lawnmower starting up.

They halted and looked at each other.

"That's torn it," Johnno murmured.

They moved the last few yards in single file and approaching the gates cautiously from the side, peered through the bars. Apart from the lawnmower driver, there were three other men working in the vicinity of the gate.

They moved past and onto a cart track that ran parallel to the wall.

Johnno looked at Brain hopefully. "What'll we do now?"

"Follow the wall around," Brain said. "There'll be another gate, more than probably. Tradesmen's entrance and stuff like that."

He turned and walked up the cart track and the others followed.

The Ant, who had invested heavily in the expedition, was beginning to get depressed. "That wall goes on for miles," he complained. "I'll bet it's longer than the Great Wall of China."

"No chance," said Johnno. "The Great Wall of China is twelve hundred miles long."

Brain looked at Johnno in surprise. "How did you know that?"

"From the *Book of Amazing Facts*," Johnno said proudly.

The Ant swiped irritably at the swarm of gnats that surrounded him. "I'm sorry I gave you that book. You're driving me barmy telling me bits out of it."

"I know what you mean," Nellie broke in. "He told me the other day that no two snowflakes were alike."

"That's what it says in the book," Johnno snapped.

Nellie shoved her perspiring face close to Johnno's. "I don't care what it says in the blinking book. It stands to reason that no one has examined every snowflake that ever fell, so how do they know?"

They were startled by a high pitched scream from Joan. Nellie turned to her. "What's wrong? Did a horsefly get you?"

Joan took a deep breath. "No," she said. "A snowflake got me. We're standing here in the middle of a heatwave, being eaten alive by every creepy crawlie in England, talking about snowflakes."

Nellie stepped into the breach. "Let's get into the shade and have the rest of our sangwiches."

The expedition cheered up a little, and a spot was chosen close to the wall and shaded by trees hanging over the top. Nellie organised the repast, and by the time the last sandwich was eaten, and the last drop of lemonade drunk, the expedition's high spirits had returned.

After a while, Brain said, "We must be getting on. We won't get any conkers lying here."

Big Davo chewed thoughtfully on a blade of grass, then said, "Yeah."

A murmur of agreement ran through the ranks, but no one moved. They lay contentedly, looking up at a cloudless sky through a tracery of leaves. Then a strange bird fluttered onto a branch and looked down at them.

"I wonder what sort of a bird that is?" the Ant said. "I've never seen one like that before."

"It's a woodpecker," Johnno sniggered. "Put your hat on."

The Ant jumped to his feet and glared at him. "I suppose you think that's funny?"

"We all thought it was funny," Nellie giggled.

The Ant made as if to speak, then stood staring down the cart track.

Big Davo levered himself onto his elbows. "What's up?"

"A riding school," the Ant reported. "Coming this way. About seven or eight of them. What'll we do?"

"We don't do anything," Brain answered. "We're having a picnic."

Johnno sat up. "The North American Plains Indian could tell if horses or buffalo were coming, simply by placing his ear to the ground." He knelt and showed them.

"Yes," he murmured after a moment. "I can hear horses coming."

"We all know there's horses coming," Big Davo snapped. "Ant just told us."

Johnno screamed and leapt to his feet.

"Something just crawled down my earhole," he shouted, offering his ear to Brain. "Have a look, mate."

Brain brushed at his cheek. "It was a little beetle. It ran out by itself."

"I don't blame it," Ant laughed. "It must have had a terrible fright in there. I'll bet it's gone home to wash its feet."

Johnno ignored everyone's amusement and probed at his ear with his little finger.

"Here," he said after a moment. "I can't see any horses."

Everyone got up and joined him. He was right, there wasn't a horse in sight.

"I tell you," the Ant said indignantly. "I saw horses."

Brain gave a shout of excitement. "Do you know what this means?"

"Yeah," Johnno snapped. "Ant's seeing things."

"A gate," Brain said, ignoring him. "There must be another gate and there's probably stables in the grounds."

Everyone picked up their possessions and hurried towards where the Ant had last seen the horses, and as Brain had predicted, there it was.

The road into the grounds had been churned up by the passing and re-passing of horses, and one of the rusted iron gates was pinned back by a wooden stake, and the other had broken at the top hinge and leaned against the wall.

They examined the immediate area for signs of activity, then moved cautiously in. They left the path and went into the trees, stopping and listening every so often. Then they came to a stand of horse-chestnuts. The conkers in their spiky pods hung from the trees and lay about in profusion on the ground. Everyone gave a delighted shout, then spent the next few minutes shushing each other. Carrier bags were opened and they applied themselves to the task of collecting conkers.

Over the next hour the expedition gradually spread out, and it was only when Brain's bags were full and his conker madness waning, that he decided it was time to round everyone up and withdraw with their loot.

Nellie and Joan were the first two he came across, their bags were full and they were beginning to feel anxious.

"Where's the others?" Brain asked.

Nellie pointed. "They went in that direction."

The three of them moved off, and found Big Davo standing in the middle of a small clearing looking depressed.

"What's up?" Nellie asked.

"There's still millions of them," Big Davo gloomed. "I wish we'd brought a handcart."

"We'd have had a little trouble getting it on the bus," Brain said. "Where's Johnno and Ant?"

"Over here," Big Davo picked up his bags and they followed him. Johnno's bags were standing under a huge tree, and high in the foliage they could hear crashing noises and grunts. "Johnno," Big Davo called.

There were more crashes and grunts, then Johnno dropped to the ground grinning in triumph and covered with a light dusting of greenfly. He had stuffed conkers down the front of his shirt and he bulged in a peculiar way.

"There was some smashing big conkers in that tree," he patted the lumps in his shirt. "I've got them here."

"You look a sight," Nellie said.

"I don't care," Johnno replied. "Are we going now?"

"As soon as we find the Ant," Brain nodded. "Any idea where he is?"

Johnno hefted his bag of conkers. "No, he was here when I climbed that tree. I don't know where he is now."

Brain looked around. "Well, he didn't pass Davo, so he must have gone this way."

They moved off carrying their conkers, and came to a path that curved through a clump of silver birch. On the path lay a couple of conkers.

"A clue," Big Davo said.

"We're getting close to the big house," Brain fretted.

They came to a wide sluggish stream and the path led to stepping stones to cross it. The stones stuck up a couple of feet, showing that the stream was usually a lot deeper, but because of the dry spell only a slick of water showed on top of the glutinous mud on the stream bed.

Nellie eyed it with distaste. "Hope I don't slip when we cross. I don't fancy landing in that."

"Me neither," Joan shuddered.

In the event, everyone got across without incident,

and once over, they could see the bulk of the big house throught the trees.

"I don't like it," Brain said. "We're too close, there's bound to be people about. Where is that idiot Ant?"

"Don't call me an idiot." Ant's voice came from overhead. Everyone looked around, and they located him high in a huge sycamore that leaned over the stream bed.

"You won't find any conkers in that tree," Johnno hissed. "It's a sycamore."

"I know," the Ant said coldly. "I'm not daft."

"That's open to debate," Brain said irritably. "Come on down and we'll get out of here before we're spotted.

"Okay," the Ant nodded, vanishing.

Then there was the sound of a branch breaking, and the Ant hurtled out of the tree clutching two handfuls of small twigs and splatted into the muddy bed of the stream.

Globules of mud flew everywhere. They shouted angrily and ran back pulling out handkerchiefs to wipe spots of mud off faces and clothes.

Then, enraged, they all ran back to the bank of the stream. For a moment nothing could be seen.

"Where is he?" Nellie whispered anxiously.

As if in reply, a large lump of mud lifted itself up off the stream bed, and lurched towards them.

"Are you all right?" Joan asked, backing away.

"Of course I am," the Ant bragged. "And I must have fallen a hundred feet."

Johnno eyed the sycamore. "Fifteen feet at the most."

The Ant glared at him, then stood with his arms outstretched, leaning forward slightly.

Big Davo examined him. "Why are you standing like that?"

"The mud's inside my shirt," the Ant explained. "It squelches when my arms touch my sides."

"They won't let you on the bus like that," Nellie said. "We'll have to clean you up somehow."

Joan nodded. "It doesn't matter about the clothes so much, they'll soon dry this weather and we can brush the mud off, but a wash is a must."

Big Davo made a wide gesture that covered the woods. "How?"

The others looked at Brain hopefully.

Brain sighed heavily and pondered. He had just had a premonition that this was the moment when everything started to go wrong. "There might be a horse trough at the back of the house," he said finally. "A lot of big old houses had them."

"That's it then," Nellie said happily. "We get the top part of him clean, and we can get him on the bus."

They moved cautiously nearer, clutching their bags of precious conkers, the Ant squelching at the rear. At the edge of the woods they paused and examined the large paved area at the back of the house.

Big Davo pointed. "A horse trough," he breathed.

They looked at Brain reverently, then Nellie said, "There's nobody about, let's get it over with."

They ran across the open space, crouching, like

soldiers in a war film, and reached the trough. It was dry, and half full of rubble.

They looked at each other, then at the mud-encrusted Ant.

"If we pull lumps of long grass, perhaps we could rub him a bit cleaner," Joan suggested.

Nellie examined the Ant again. "No chance," she said.

Once again everyone looked expectantly at Brain. The feeling of gloom that had enveloped him, deepened to such an extent that he decided to meet disaster halfway.

"We'll knock at the kitchen door," he said, "and ask."

Breaths were sucked in, but as Brain was striding towards the house, they had no choice but to follow him.

He reached the door, put his bags of conkers against the wall and knocked. The door swung open. He stood a moment, then stepped inside. The kitchen was empty and under the window stood a big old-fashioned sink. He called to the others, who were poised for flight.

"The kitchen's empty and there's a sink. Let's get him in, wash him and get him out."

The Ant was bundled into the kitchen and Johnno and Big Davo pulled his shirt off.

Nellie put the plug in and turned the taps on, testing the water with her fingers. "Look around for something to dry him on," she asked Joan.

Johnno and Big Davo shoved the Ant towards the sink.

"I can wash myself," he snarled.

"It'll be quicker if we all help," Big Davo soothed.

Then Nellie glimpsed a movement through the window over the sink. "Someone's coming," she hissed.

There was a moment of wild panic with everyone running around, bumping into each other. Then Johnno spotted a flight of stairs at the far end of the kitchen. "This way," he called.

They raced up the stairs in a bunch, the door at the top was open, but as they reached it they heard the sound of voices. Lurching to a halt, they stood with hearts pounding. Then Brain noticed a small cupboard at the side of the stairs. He grabbed at the door knob and it opened.

"In here," he gasped, shoving Nellie and Joan before him.

Big Davo followed, and when Johnno squeezed in, the press of bodies stopped the door from closing. He had to pull back on the doorknob to stop it from flying open again.

They crowded together, listening, then Johnno let go of the door with one hand and clutched at his stomach.

"What's wrong?" Big Davo whispered.

"A button just popped off my shirt and all my conkers are coming through the gap," Johnno whispered hoarsely.

"Just hang on to that door," Big Davo pleaded.

"I wonder where the Ant is?" Joan whispered. "He's not with us."

"I don't know," Brain was squashed between Nellie

and Big Davo. "And I don't care. If it wasn't for that lunatic, we wouldn't be in this cupboard."

When the others had raced for the stairs, Ant had wasted several precious seconds flailing about looking for his shirt. By the time he had found it, the others had vanished. He looked around wildly, and spotted what he took to be a small empty cupboard in the wall. He jumped in, curled up and shut the doors. He had heard someone come into the kitchen, and he listened, heart pounding. Up above him he could also hear voices.

Mr Mywell, the administrator in charge of the Advanced Education courses, was a happy man. He knew every beam and brick of the old building, and all its history. Normally, the teachers taking the weekend courses were British, and as most of them had visited similar old houses around the country, they were inclined to be indifferent.

This time however, the group contained an American teacher on an exchange visit, and he was fascinated. His interest and intelligent questions had inspired Mr Mywell, and in consequence he could feel the rest of the group becoming interested despite themselves.

"This," said Mr Mywell, opening a door and gesturing them inside. "Is what you might call a serving room. The dining room is connected to this room, and the food from the kitchen was hauled up a service shaft by hand, so that it would still be hot when it reached the dining table."

He strode across the room with the teachers following. "I'll show you how it worked."

Set into the wall was a large iron wheel, and close to it, two small doors. Mr Mywell flipped open the doors, revealing a shaft. Then he grasped the wheel and began to turn it.

"Odd," he grunted over the click of a ratchet. "It seems to be stiff today."

The teachers watched as a small compartment came into view, then sucked in their breath in surprise as they saw its occupant. A mud encrusted creature clutching a filthy rag. The foetid odour of river mud wafted towards them.

The Ant was equally horrified as he stared at the group facing him. His horror increased when he recognised Mr Seymour and Mr Thomas. He attempted an ingratiating smile. To the onlookers it looked like a threatening snarl, and they backed nervously away.

Unaware of the drama, Mr Mywell removed the ratchet and started lowering the compartment down to the kitchen.

The Ant, still smiling gamely, disappeared from view.

"What was that?" whispered the American teacher.

Mr Seymour and Mr Thomas exchanged glances and both shouted, "Hopkins!"

"What's a Hopkin?" the American asked.

Mr Mywell lost control of the wheel and the compartment dropped the last few yards.

The sound of the crash echoed up the shaft, followed by the sound of a woman screaming.

"Where's the kitchen?" Mr Seymour asked the bewildered Mr Mywell.

Mr Mywell pointed. "The last door on your right."

Mr Seymour and Mr Thomas charged from the room with the others following. They raced down the stairs into the kitchen as a pack.

They found the cook clinging to a table for support. She pointed. "It ran under the sink."

Mr Thomas lunged under the sink and emerged with the Ant. The cook screamed again. "What is it?" she asked.

"It's a Hopkin," the American teacher said knowledgeably. He studied Mr Thomas's captive. "Ugly brutes."

In the small silence, as the teachers contemplated the Ant, there was the sound of a cupboard door creaking open, and a muffled exclamation.

They turned as one and witnessed a stream of horse-chestnuts bouncing down the stairs.

Mr Seymour exchanged another brief glance with Mr Thomas, then trod warily up the stairs. At the top, the cupboard door was gently closing itself again. Mr Seymour snatched it open and peered inside.

"Hello, sir," Nellie Allbright said.

When the explanations were over and Mr Mywell had gathered his flock around him again, he announced lunch would be served shortly and brought them to the dining room. While they waited, small groups formed, discussing recent events.

"What I can't understand," said the American

teacher, "is why they wanted these horse-chestnuts. What did they call them?"

"Conkers," another teacher answered. "It's a seasonal game."

"OK," said the American. "But how do you play it?"

His question aroused childhood memories, and everyone started explaining at once. Then another of the teachers restored order and some conkers were brought from the kitchen. A pipesmoker bored a hole in them with the probe on his penknife, and string was pushed through and knotted. Two teachers faced each other clutching the conkers, and another elected himself spokesman.

"Supposing," said the spokesman, "that the conker season is a week or two old, and his conker has smashed eight others. That conker is then known as an eighter. If his opponent's conker has smashed five, it's a fiver. Now if the eighter smashes the fiver it then becomes a thirteener."

He looked at the American teacher anxiously. "Do you understand?"

The American nodded. "They don't look tough enough to last that long."

"There are all sorts of tricks," the spokesman explained. "Soaking them in vinegar, baking them in an oven. They all have their own secret methods of hardening them. Now for the demonstration."

He nodded at the teachers with the conkers. One held his at arm's length, the other took a pace back and judged his distance. Everyone watched intently. The conker hissed down in a wild arc and struck his opponent a vicious crack on the knuckles.

The unfortunate dropped his conker and, thrusting his injured hand under his armpit, began to stamp in small circles.

"Do you think it might catch on in the States?" asked the spokesman.

"I doubt it," said the American.

Mr Seymour drove his car carefully through the crowded village market crowds, and turned into a fairly traffic-free lane.

The gloom of the Great Conker Expedition members could almost be felt.

"Enjoy your tea?" Mr Seymour ventured.

"It was lovely, sir," Joan replied dully.

There was another gloomy pause. Then the Ant broke the silence.

"That lady nearly pulled my ears off when she was getting the mud out of them," he said bitterly. "And that was after I'd had a shower. I'd got most of it out anyway."

"She washed and dried your clothes," Mr Seymour pointed out.

"That was nice of her," the Ant admitted.

"Never mind your blinking clothes," Johnno broke in. "What about our conkers?"

"We had loads, sir," Big Davo said. "You should have seen them."

"Twelve carrier bags full," Mr Seymour nodded. "Quite a haul."

Brain looked at him sharply. "How do you know how many bags there were, sir?"

"I saw them by the wall outside the kitchen," Mr Seymour grinned. "I managed to get six of them in the boot of my car. Mr Thomas will collect the other six. You can get them on Monday at school."

"You're a luvly feller, sir," Nellie breathed, as the gloom lifted.

"I know," Mr Seymour admitted shamelessly.

7

Taking the first lesson on the Monday after the Great Conker Expedition, Mr Seymour noticed that the expedition members were being unusually attentive, and when the opportunity arose, favoured him with beaming smiles.

He realised that he had incurred their gratitude and in consequence began to feel somewhat uneasy.

The code of 2D was not unlike the Mafia. When you owed, you paid. He had been nice to them, and they were going to be nice right back at him, as soon as the occasion presented itself.

At dinner that morning he was on playground duty when he saw Mr Thomas being escorted to his car by the expedition members, who were intent on claiming their conkers. They fussed around him like tugs around a liner.

Mr Seymour got considerable comfort from the realisation that they were grateful to Mr Thomas too.

He watched them set up shop by the bicycle sheds and they were soon surrounded by eager customers.

Mr Seymour wandered off, pausing to chat here and there, and it was a little over half an hour later when he had circled the school and came in view of the bicycle sheds again. The crowd had gone and the conker magnates were tipping the remainder of the conkers into one bag. When they were finished it was only half full.

Johnno, who lived nearest, was entrusted with the bag, as he could get back before afternoon school started.

"Hello, sir," said Johnno, moving past Mr Seymour.

"What about the other six bags, Johnstone?" Mr Seymour asked.

"Brain said not to bring them, sir," Johnno replied. "They might wet things."

Mr Seymour stared at his retreating back, then looked hopefully at Brain.

"Flood the market, sir," Brain grinned.

"Smart move," Mr Seymour approved.

Brain looked thoughtful. "I wish I'd brought nails to make holes in the conkers, and string too, sir. They'd have sold well."

"You can't think of everything," Mr Seymour consoled.

As the week progressed, Mr Seymour noticed that the members of 2D who were grateful to him seemed somewhat preoccupied. He guessed correctly that they were busy with their business commitments and the demand for conkers, though steady, had slowed a little.

Realising it would be a few days at least before their gratitude manifested itself, he began to relax a little.

During the week he was in the teachers' room having a cup of tea and chatting with Mr Thomas and

Miss Lomax, when the headmaster bustled in with a stranger.

"Your attention, please," he called. "I have some exciting news."

Talk stopped as the teachers examined Mr Belham's companion. He was tall and very pale, and wore the expression of a man who had just put his foot into something unpleasant.

"This is Percival Gratton, a leading art critic," Mr Belham went on. "He has been judging the paintings in the art competition organised by the local paper. It seems that two of our pupils have won. Mr Gratton is very impressed. I'll let him explain."

Mr Belham gestured the art critic forward.

Percival Gratton nodded and drifted languidly to the centre of the room.

"When I was asked by your local paper to judge the paintings," he began, "I never for a moment imagined I would find such exciting talent." He put a flat carrying case on the table and tapped it with his forefinger. "When I think of the artistic ability going to waste in schools all over the country, it saddens me."

Mr Gamboge put down his cup and saucer with a clatter and stood up. "There is no artistic talent going to waste in this school," he said coldly.

"Really?" Mr Gratton sneered. He opened the carrying case and took out two paintings. "Then you will not be surprised when I tell you the winners' names."

Conscious of the attention he was getting, he took his time putting on a pair of rimless glasses. Then glancing triumphantly around the room, he announced, "Helen Allbright and Anthony Hopkins."

Mr Gamboge's legs buckled and he sat down again. There was a mass intake of breath from the other teachers.

Mr Gratton looked pleased with the result his announcement had caused.

"I've surprised you all," he smirked.

"You have no idea how much," said Mr Seymour.

The headmaster cleared his throat. "May we see these masterpieces, please?"

Mr Gratton took a painting out of the case and held it up. "This is by Helen Allbright, and is a painting of a wedding. The style is primitive, but notice the black bars running down the painting. The child obviously regards the bride and groom as being in prison. She is saying that they are no longer free. It is entitled, 'The wedding'."

He held it for a few moments more, then placed it reverently on the table. The next painting he looked at for a few moments before showing it.

"This is really magnificent," he announced. " 'A sunset', by Anthony Hopkins. A brilliant abstract. Notice the whirling kaleidoscope of colour. It screams sunset at you. It is the result of keen observation." The teachers stared at it open-mouthed.

"It looks like the result of an explosion in a paint factory," Mr Thomas growled.

Miss Lomax muffled a giggle.

"You are a Philistine," Mr Gratton sneered.

"I'm a Welshman," said Mr Thomas.

Mr Belham stepped forward hastily. "I understand you want to meet these children?"

"That," said Mr Gratton, "is the purpose of my visit."

Ignoring the teachers, Mr Gratton examined the paintings anew, humming tunelessly to himself.

Mr Belham opened the door and looked up and down the corridor. A dreamy bespectacled youth came into view, eating a bag of crisps.

"Earnshaw," Mr Belham snapped. "Come into the teachers' room immediately."

The youth started nervously and began to choke on the crisps he was munching.

Mr Belham tut-tutted irritably, and turned back into the teachers' room.

Mr Gratton was still examining the paintings intently, and in turn was being watched with equal intentness by the teachers. Mr Belham spun around to step out into the corridor and bumped into the nervous Earnshaw. Both jumped and leapt backwards.

"I haven't done anything, sir," Earnshaw pleaded. "I never do anything."

"I know," Mr Belham snapped. "I believe I said as much on your last school report. I want you to find Helen Allbright and Anthony Hopkins, and tell them to come to the teachers' room immediately."

"Yes, sir," Earnshaw beamed. He glanced past the headmaster into the room.

"*Now*, Earnshaw," Mr Belham growled.

"Yes, sir," Earnshaw said again, vanishing rapidly.

* * *

Nellie and the Ant were with the others, selling conkers by the bicycle sheds.

"You've got to go to the teachers' room and see Mr Belham right away," said Earnshaw, the glad bearer of grim tidings.

"Did he say why?" Nellie asked.

"No," Earnshaw admitted. "But there was a tall skinny feller in the room looking at some paintings."

Nellie and the Ant looked at him blankly, but Joan Alison gave a little scream and said, "Nellie, the painting competition in the art class, remember?"

Nellie and the Ant paled.

"Oh heck," said Johnno and Big Davo together.

"It won't be that," Brain said firmly. "It wasn't schoolwork, it was a competition. If your painting's spoilt, you just don't win and that's it."

The Ant and Nellie looked at him hopefully.

"Are you sure?" Nellie asked.

"I'm positive," said Brain.

Ant squared his shoulders. "Come on, Nellie, let's find out."

"I'll come too," Joan said. "It was my fault as well."

The Ant and Nellie tried to dissuade her, but she was adamant. The others looked thoughtful as they watched them walk towards the school.

"I'll bet they're in big trouble," Earnshaw said cheerfully.

Big Davo, Johnno and Brain turned and glared at him.

"How," Big Davo asked, "would you like to wake up with a crowd around you?"

Earnshaw, who knew when he was not wanted, beat a hasty retreat.

By unspoken consent, the trio closed up shop and made for the school buildings, intending to be near the teachers' room if sympathy were needed.

Mr Belham saw Nellie in the doorway and said, "Come in, come in. Is Hopkins with you?"

The Ant emerged from behind Nellie's sturdy frame.

"Good," Mr Belham beamed. He stood between Nellie and the Ant, and led them forward with a friendly hand on their shoulders.

"Here they are, Mr Gratton," he called.

"Ah," Mr Gratton sighed. "My artists."

Mr Belham noticed Joan. "I didn't send for you, Joan," he said.

"I know, sir," Joan replied, her face pale. "But I'm responsible too."

"Responsible?" Mr Belham began.

"Please," Mr Gratton hissed. "This is a moment to remember. I want silence."

Mr Belham closed his eyes and took a deep breath. The teachers cheered up and exchanged knowing little elbow nudges.

Mr Gratton picked up a painting and faced Nellie. "You are Helen Allbright?" he asked.

Nellie nodded warily.

Mr Gratton smiled fondly at her. "It delights me

to tell you that you have won first prize in the girls' section of the painting competition." He put the painting down and picked up the other. "And you," he said to the Ant, "have won the boys' section with this magnificent abstract."

Nellie, the Ant and Joan looked pathetically at Mr Gamboge.

"You have both won the competition," Mr Gamboge confirmed.

Nellie looked bewildered. "But our paintings were ruined, sir. The Ant drew black lines down mine."

"He didn't," Mr Gamboge tried to look shocked. "Why, Hopkins?"

"Because she splashed red paint on my face," the Ant complained. "And on my painting. Then they squiggled all different colours on it, and messed it up. Just look at it."

"They?" Mr Gamboge queried, fighting a smile. "Were you involved, Joan?"

"Yes, sir," Joan murmured nervously. "I painted a moustache, too."

The teachers examined the paintings with renewed interest.

"Where did you paint the moustache, Joan?" Mr Seymour queried.

"On his face, sir," she said, pointing to the Ant.

"I had a terrible job getting it off, sir," the Ant complained. "And the spots, too."

"I just shook the brush, sir," Nellie explained. "I'd no idea it had gone on his face."

The Ant looked hopefully at Mr Gamboge. "They

71

must have been good paintings in the first place if they won a prize even when they were ruined."

"That is very true," said Mr Gamboge, who looked like a man at peace with the world. He had taken a great dislike to Mr Gratton.

"We will still get our prize, won't we, sir?" Nellie asked anxiously.

"I shall see to it personally, Nellie," Mr Gamboge purred. He turned to Mr Gratton who was looking horrified.

"Do you have about your person a list of prizes, so that my pupils can make a choice?"

Mr Gratton fumbled in his pockets and thrust a pamphlet into Mr Gamboge's outstretched hand. Then he glanced at his watch.

"Good heavens, is that the time?" he muttered. "I must hurry or I'll miss my train." He favoured the grinning teachers with a sickly smile and hurried from the room.

Mr Gamboge handed Nellie the prize list. "When you both have picked your prizes, let me know," he said.

Mr Belham opened the door for them. "Off you go."

They looked at the headmaster anxiously, trying to guess his mood.

"We didn't mean to spoil the paintings, sir," Nellie said.

"Of course not." Mr Belham patted her shoulder.

"It just happened, sir," the Ant explained.

"Undoubtedly," the headmaster beamed, ruffling his hair. He ushered them gently into the corridor and closed the door. They stood a moment, bewildered. Then they heard roars of laughter from the teachers' room.

"Grown-ups are definitely barmy," the Ant stated. "I wonder if I'll be barmy when I grow up?"

"You're in with a chance," Nellie giggled. "You're barmy now."

8

Nellie still hadn't made up her mind which prize to choose when she and Joan went to help their mothers at the Mothers Union jumble sale. As a result she was rather preoccupied as she and Joan set up the tables and helped put the jumble out. Joan looked at her curiously a couple of times but said nothing. It was very close to the opening time when Nellie noticed that one of the tables was covered in young plants. They were in pots, paper cups and old margarine cartons. In the centre of the table was a large aspidistra in a glazed earthenware pot.

"Joan," Nellie hissed, suddenly grasping her arm. "What have I been thinking of?"

"I was wondering," Joan said dryly. "Tell me."

Nellie pointed. "Look at that luvly aspidistra, and all those other plants. We could buy some for Mr Seymour as a present, because he was nice about the conkers, and for giving us a lift home."

"It's a good idea," Joan admitted. "But what about Mr Thomas? He was nice too."

"I don't know what he likes," Nellie said, moving towards the flower stall. "I know Mr Seymour likes gardening because I heard him and Mr Dickens talking about a greenhouse they were building."

The lady in charge of the table let them have the aspidistra and the other assorted potted plants at a very reasonable price.

Nellie and Joan put them in the cloakroom, then buckled down to help again, glowing with satisfaction.

When everything was ready, Nellie and Joan were thanked for their help and told that they could go. This insistence on their departure stemmed from a previous charity jumble sale opened by a visiting dignitary, who had carelessly thrown her fur coat and handbag on a table while she mingled, and had returned to find that Nellie had sold the coat for 50p and Joan had made 25p on the handbag. The purchasers had not left the premises when the loss was discovered and the brawl that followed had become a local legend.

"How will we get this lot to Mr Seymour?" Joan asked, when the door had shut again.

"I'll mind the plants," Nellie said. "You run down to the waste ground at the bottom of Gladstone Street. The lads usually go there to kick a football around on Saturday. Tell them we need a hand here."

Mr Seymour had just finished a hectic week having his drive widened and was scraping up mortar and bits of broken bricks from around his new gateposts, when the aspidistra came into view, followed by a chorus of, "Hello, sir."

"This is a surprise," Mr Seymour said, leaning his spade against the wall and coming over to them.

Nellie had a quick glance around. "I hope we haven't come at a bad time," she said courteously. "But we brought you these plants. I hope you like them."

"I certainly do," Mr Seymour smiled.

The aspidistra lowered itself to the ground, revealing Johnno's sweating face.

"This one's not half heavy, sir," he panted. "We took turns carrying it here."

Mr Seymour picked it up. "Come on around the back, I'll give the plants a drop of water, then you can have a sit down and a glass of lemonade."

At the back of the house Mrs Seymour turned from her task of pruning the roses and came towards them.

"Oh, what a beautiful aspidistra," she said, endearing herself to Nellie. "I haven't seen one for years, I thought they were extinct."

Within minutes Mrs Seymour had set up a table on the lawn and produced a jug of iced lemonade and a tray of cakes.

By the time Mr Seymour had seen to the plants, the plate was empty and the last of the lemonade was being savoured. Nellie brushed some crumbs off her dress and stood up. The others drained their glasses and did the same.

"That was luvly, sir, thank you," Nellie said.

"The plants was the girls' presents, sir," Big Davo explained. "We only helped carry them."

"We're still thinking about ours," Johnno butted in.

"It'll be something special," the Ant bragged.

They waved goodbye to Mrs Seymour, and Mr Seymour walked with them to the gate.

Big Davo eyed the posts. "They still need those concrete tops on, don't they, sir?"

"Pillar caps," Mr Seymour said. "Yes, but the only ones available are the ordinary flat ones. My wife fancies the ones with the stone ball on top, but they don't seem to make them any more." Brain moved forward and examined the pillars intently, then when they had left Mr Seymour, he walked behind the others smiling to himself.

Johnno turned and studied Brain's face.

"Here," he cried. "You've had an idea, haven't you?"

The others stopped and gathered around him expectantly.

"Well," Brain began. "You know those old houses by the canal bridge?"

"They've been flattened," the Ant objected.

"Yes," said Brain. "But they haven't moved the rubble yet, and when we were playing there the other day, I saw a pillar cap with a stone ball on it lying in the grass. Now there were six houses and they all had those pillar caps, that means there are eleven more lying somewhere, there's bound to be at least one unbroken."

They considered his idea. Then Big Davo said, "Will they be the right size, though?"

"I think so," Brain replied. "I'll know for sure when I see the one in the grass."

"Me and Joan will help," Nellie said.

"It's our present," Johnno cautioned.

"You helped with ours," Nellie snapped.

"That's true," said Johnno. Then he shouted, "Here's the bus."

They all raced for the bus stop and clambered upstairs, breathless.

"They'll be blooming heavy to carry," Big Davo carried on the conversation when they were settled. "We'll have to get a cart or a wheelbarrow."

"I don't fancy pushing a wheelbarrow all the way to Mr Seymour's," Johnno said.

"We don't have to," Brain answered. "All we have to do is get them as far as the school. We hide them somewhere, then Mr Seymour can put them in the boot of his car on Monday."

"What about trollies?" Joan asked.

Most of the lads had made trollies. They were made from old pram wheels, big wheels at the back, smaller ones at the front, and steered with a rope attached to the front axle.

"Mine is broken," said the Ant.

"So is mine," Johnno gloomed. "And Davo's got pinched."

"I've made a new one," Big Davo said proudly. "I found an old pram on the tip and the wheels were in good nick. My dad helped me. It goes wide at the back where you sit. It's a smasher."

"That's it then," Brain announced. "We'll go around after our tea and pick up the one I saw lying in the grass. That'll do for starters."

Big Davo's trolley was admired by everyone, and

he let them take turns riding in it all the way to their destination.

The rubble of the houses had been pushed into high mounds by a bulldozer and swarmed with children. Brain led them past the rubble and into what had been the gardens. He found one unbroken pillar cap without any trouble, and between them they got it on the trolley with much grunting and cries of, "Mind your fingers."

"Shall we all have a look around, to see if we can find another?" Johnno asked.

Brain studied the crowds on the mounds. Some faces were familiar, but there were too many strangers. If it became known they needed a pillar cap, some opportunist might find one and demand a swap for it, or offer to sell it to them.

"No," he decided. "It's best if no one knows we want one."

They all nodded, understanding what he meant.

"Tomorrow will be best," Nellie said, "it being Sunday, but we must get here early."

Once off the rough ground of the garden, the trolley ran effortlessly with two of them pulling on the steering rope and one pushing. They took turns about until they reached the school.

On their way to a gap in the railings, known to the pupils as the "players' entrance", they saw a side gate open. This was a great advantage, but it meant that Mr Croft was about somewhere. The Ant went in and reconnoitred. After a few minutes he appeared and pointed to the boilerhouse, then signalled them to come in. They raced across the playground, everyone either pushing or pulling. The tricky part was moving between the boilerhouse and the gymnasium on their way to the car park, but with the Ant keeping a wary eye open, they managed.

They left the pillar cap lying flat on the corner of the low wall that separated the car park from the playground. It was difficult to see unless you were close to it, and they felt pleased with themselves as they waited for the Ant to signal again.

When the signal came, they moved quietly past Mr Croft's lair, and then they raced out of the school, stopping breathless but triumphant when they were well clear. Johnno grinned at the others. "One to go," he panted.

They met early on Sunday morning and waited for Big Davo. When he showed up there was a plastic bag on his trolley.

"What's in that?" Johnno asked, poking it.

"Baby clothes," Big Davo said gloomily. "I've got to take them to my Auntie Madge. They were for my sister, but she grew so fast most of them aren't even worn."

"Has your auntie got a new baby?" Joan asked. Big Davo nodded.

"Can we have a look at it?" Nellie pleaded.

"I'll ask," Big Davo said indulgently. "Do you want to come with us? It won't take long if we take turns on my trolley, you can hold the bag on with your legs, it's tied at the top."

It was a warm humid day and they arrived at Big

Davo's auntie's lathered in sweat. The front door was open, but Big Davo knocked and, hefting the bag, strode in calling, "Auntie Madge".

The others heard someone shushing him, then after a minute or two he came out and said to Nellie and Joan, "You can come in and look at the baby if you want. I've just woke it, but it's not crying." Nellie and Joan followed him in.

Brain, Johnno and the Ant sat side by side on the length of the trolley and waited.

Big Davo came out and sat on the doorstep facing them. "I don't suppose any of you want to see it?" he said.

The lads shook their heads.

"Is it a boy or a girl?" Brain asked.

Big Davo scratched his head. 'I forgot to ask. I think it must be a girl though, if my mam's sent around my sister's gear."

"I don't think it matters much what they wear when they're new," Brain said.

"I wouldn't know," Big Davo admitted.

"They look like boiled monkeys at first," Johnno broke in. "At least my sister did, but after a month or two they get nice faces."

Having exhausted the subject of new born babies, they sat in a companionable silence for a while, then Johnno scratched his close cropped red hair and said irritably, "What's keeping those girls?"

"They're looking at the baby," Big Davo reminded him.

"How long does it take to look at a baby," Johnno

asked. Then to Big Davo, "Go in and tell them to hurry up."

"He'd be wasting his time," said the Ant, who suffered from sisters. "If you ask them to hurry up they take longer for spite."

"You're right," Big Davo agreed. He had observed the same phenomena himself.

There was another short silence, then Nellie and Joan emerged. Big Davo stood to let them pass.

"He's luvly," Nellie sighed.

"Gorgeous," Joan agreed.

"It's a boy," Big Davo said to Brain.

"Go to the top of the class," Brain grinned.

Johnno stood and rubbed his hands. "Whose turn is it on the trolley?" he asked hopefully.

"Ant's," Brain answered.

"Are you sure?"

"Positive," Brain said firmly.

"So am I." The Ant settled himself on the trolley and wrapped the steering rope around his hands. He eyed the road ahead of him. "A nice little slope. I should get a good head of steam up."

Big Davo and Brain began pushing, and the others trotted alongside. The trolley began to pick up speed.

"About three streets down," Big Davo instructed, "turn right, you'll see a shop on the corner."

They stopped pushing and ran behind. The trolley began to pull ahead. The gap increased and the Ant swung into the third road down and saw, to his horror, it had no exit but two narrow entries that forked like the letter "Y".

To add to his troubles the road had been tarred over the original granite blocks and was potholed. Big Davo and the others ran into the street as he was halfway along it.

Big Davo's eyes widened. "Oh heck, I'd forgotten about that." He cupped his hands around his mouth and shouted, "Turn left." The Ant, bouncing and rattling along at an increasing speed, heard him shout.

"Left?" he screamed, wanting confirmation.

"Right," Big Davo shouted back.

The Ant reached the end of the road and turned right.

Big Davo's shoulders slumped. "I could bite my tongue out," he said, to no one in particular.

The sound of a crash came up the street, and they all began running.

"What's he hit?" Johnno asked.

"A brick wall," Big Davo mourned. "That entry is blocked off."

They found the Ant lying beside the trolley. Big Davo and Johnno pulled it away from him, and Brain, Nellie and Joan helped him to his feet. He shook his head in a dazed manner, then looked at the wall he had hit.

"How long has that wall been there?" he asked.

Brain glared at it. "About a hundred years."

The Ant glanced at Big Davo. "Why did you tell me to turn right?"

"I didn't," Big Davo protested. "I shouted left, then you shouted left, so I shouted right. Meaning *right*, turn left."

The Ant looked at Big Davo thoughtfully. "Do you think you could explain that to me again in about an hour, when my head's stopped spinning?"

He took a tentative step forward.

"Your knee's cut," Nellie said.

"I'm lucky my legs aren't broken," the Ant complained bitterly.

"Is the trolley all right?"

"The two front wheels are like duck eggs," Johnno replied. He picked up the trolley and turned it around, pulling it out of the entry by the steering rope. The wheels were now oval in shape, and the front end of the trolley rose and fell each time they turned.

The others followed, and the Ant limped after them.

"If your leg's still hurting, mate," Big Davo said to the Ant, "you can ride on the trolley."

"If anyone rides on that now, they'll finish up seasick," the Ant said coldly. Then he relented at the miserable look on Big Davo's face as he looked at his trolley. "I've got a good pair of front wheels you can have, I've been waiting to find the big back wheels, but they don't seem to make those sort of prams any more."

"The point is," Brain broke in. "The trolley will still carry the other pillar cap if we can find one. Then we can put Ant's wheels on and it'll be as good as new."

Big Davo joined Johnno on the steering rope, and with no one riding, they soon came to their destination. Apart from a couple of small children playing on a mound of sand, the site was deserted. They hid the trolley under some bushes, and spread out.

Johnno found a pillar cap but there was no stone ball on it, just a hollow where it had been.

Brain examined it. "They must have moulded the cap and ball separately," he said. "The bottom of the hollow is flat, so the bottom of the ball will be flat. It must have come out when the workmen knocked the gateposts over."

"We'll have to look for the ball, then." Big Davo ducked under the bushes and put the pillar cap on the trolley.

"Unless we find a complete one."

"No chance," the Ant grunted. "We've been all over. If there are any around, they're under that lot." He jerked his thumb at the mounds of rubble.

"One more try." Brain suggested.

They looked at each other and shrugged. Then they spread out and began moving towards the mounds of rubble again.

The Ant said, "Hang on a minute, where are the girls?"

"They said there were enough people looking through the rubble, and they'd look through the gardens."

There was a cracking of branches in the bushes facing them, and Joan and Nellie emerged. There was mud on their shoes and socks, but Nellie was clutching a stone ball.

"This is all we could find," Joan said. "Is it any good?"

"Girls," Brain replied, as Big Davo took the heavy stone ball from Nellie. "You are a couple of marvels."

Johnno and Ant dragged the trolley over, and Big Davo placed the stone ball in the recess. It fitted perfectly. "A trowelful of sand and cement and it'll be as good as new," Big Davo said.

Johnno pulled on the steering rope and started the trolley moving. "Let's get it to the school, and then we can fix the new wheels on."

Progress was slow because of the eccentric movement of the wheels. Eventually they reached the school and made their way to the widest of the players' entrances. Nellie and Joan were left to mind the trolley, while the boys struggled through with the pillar cap and ball.

"Have a scout around, Ant," Brain said. "Just to be on the safe side."

The Ant nodded and limped off. Brain and Johnno carried the cap between them, walking sideways like crabs. Behind them, Big Davo carried the stone ball.

When they came around the end of the gymnasium, the Ant limped towards them, waving them back.

Brain and Johnno put the gate caps down with grunts of relief. Big Davo stood clutching the stone ball. "What's wrong?" he asked.

"Mr Croft is in the car park talking to some man," the Ant reported.

"Who is he?" Johnno asked.

"Hang on," the Ant said sarcastically. "I'll go and ask him."

Big Davo put the stone ball down by the cap. "You'd think he'd have Sunday off," he complained.

"I think he's paid to come in for a quick look

around," Brain said. "We'll have to hide them some-where else. I'll pick a spot. Won't be long."

Within minutes he was back. "Come on, lads," he said. "I've got just the place." He helped Johnno pick up the pillar cap and moved round to the side of the boilerhouse, where close to the wall the grass grew long. The pillar cap was stood up on edge against the wall, and when the long grass was pushed up again by Brain and Johnno, it was hidden.

"What about the ball?" Big Davo complained.

"Just put it down anywhere, we'll bend the grass over it. No one will come this way between now and Monday morning."

Big Davo did as he was bid, and the stone ball was quickly hidden.

"Mission accomplished," the Ant said. "Let's get back to the girls."

After a cautious glance at the car park and Mr Croft, they moved off.

9

Brain, Johnno and the Ant came into the playground on Monday morning, and homed in on the tall lanky figure of Big Davo. He was talking to Nellie and Joan.

"They're still here," he reported. "The girls got here early and had a look."

"When will we tell Mr Seymour?" the Ant asked.

"We've got basketball with Miss Lomax first lesson," Nellie said. "And you're down for PT with Mr Thomas in the gym."

Brain eyed the towering black clouds building up over Wales and Cheshire. "We'll all finish up in the gym," he predicted. "Look at that lot. It'll be lashing down soon."

"We've got Mr Seymour for the next lesson after gym, we could hang back when the bell goes and tell him then," Johnno suggested.

The idea was adopted, and they moved towards the school in anticipation of the first bell.

In the teachers' room, the headmaster confirmed Brain's prediction. "It looks like the dry spell will soon be over," he said. "You had better move your class into the gym with Mr Thomas, Miss Lomax."

The first bell went and the teachers began to move

from the room. Mr Seymour, who had a free period, sat leisurely sipping a cup of tea.

The headmaster looked at the black clouds through the staffroom window and waited until he and Mr Seymour were alone.

"I'd like your advice, Mr Seymour," he said abruptly. "I had a phone call yesterday from the Education Authorities. It seems that a TV company want to use the school to make a film. They say they'll be less than a week making it, and will cause as little inconvenience as possible. Someone will be dropping by today to give me the details. It's been left for me to decide if I should give them permission."

"Then what's the problem, headmaster?" Mr Seymour asked.

"I don't want it to interfere with their studies," Mr Belham explained. "They'll think of nothing but the filming while the TV company is here, and they'll spend the next week talking about it."

Mr Seymour put his cup down. "Possibly," he said. "But if you refuse permission and the pupils find out about it, they'll be highly indignant and will probably spend the next couple of weeks brooding."

"It's hard to know what to do," the headmaster admitted.

"Stop worrying about it until you have more information," Mr Seymour advised.

There was a quick rap on the door and Mr Croft came into the room. "Ah, there you are, Mr Belham. I've been looking for you. I was having a quick look around yesterday and I smelled gas in the kitchens. I phoned the gas board and they sent a man out. The leak was in a section of pipe running along the skirting where they stack the milk crates. The pipe was all marked where the crates had been hitting it, and the gas-board man said it would probably happen again if the pipe wasn't protected."

Mr Belham made a note on his clipboard pad. "I'll phone the Council and ask them to send a man around to box the pipe in."

At that moment there was a great crash of thunder and the rain began lashing down; huge heavy drops that bounced as they hit the ground.

The three men moved to the window and gazed out.

Within minutes the hollows in the playground became ponds, which merged and became small lakes.

"This will do my garden the world of good," Mr Seymour said cheerfully.

After about ten minutes it eased into gusty light showers, although the distant growl of thunder promised more heavy rain.

"I'll get over to the gym while I have a chance," Mr Croft said. "I'll pick up my oilskins, too, they're in the boilerhouse." He hurried from the room.

The headmaster turned from the window, his face still worried. "It's possible that a couple of million people will see this school if a television film is made. I would like to give them a good impression."

"Naturally," said Mr Seymour. "Why shouldn't they get a good impression?"

"Perhaps," Mr Belham began hesitantly, "2D will become involved. I mean they might want to film them. I know the class is well intentioned, but whenever anyone tries to organise them for any purpose, they become a perambulating disaster area."

"You are worrying unnecessarily," Mr Seymour soothed.

"Perhaps so," Mr Belham said gloomily, turning back to the window. The hunched figure of Mr Croft could be seen scuttling along the paved edge of the playground towards his boilerhouse. The headmaster gazed at him morosely. "Then there's Mr Croft. Supposing he insists on doing his bird imitations, what will people think?"

Mr Seymour burst out laughing. "There is a perfectly rational explanation for his behaviour."

"Really?" Mr Belham sounded unconvinced. He opened the window and looked up at the looming black clouds. "This is in for the day," he predicted.

The object of their discussion vanished from sight, heading for his boilerhouse. The heavy rain had flattened the high grass close to the wall, and Mr Croft saw a round white object and took it for a football left out by one of the pupils.

"Careless young devils," he muttered, giving it a playful kick.

In the teachers' room, Mr Belham was about to close the window when Mr Croft came into view again, uttering hoarse croaks and holding one leg with both hands. He progressed across the playground in a series of enormous splashing hops, slowing to a halt in the middle of one of the larger lakes.

"He's at it again, Mr Seymour," Mr Belham said in gloomy triumph.

Mr Croft stood one legged, his head sunk on his chest.

The headmaster studied him. "A heron this time, I fancy."

The rain became heavier, but Mr Croft remained motionless. "He's damned good," Mr Belham admitted reluctantly.

At break later that morning, Mr Seymour came into the teachers' room with barely enough time left for the usual cup of tea.

"I'd given you up for lost," Mr Thomas said to him. "Where have you been?"

Mr Seymour lifted the teapot and felt it cautiously. "The conker kings of 2D presented me with two pillar caps. I've been putting them in the boot of my car," he explained. He poured a cup of tea. "I'm almost certain they're the right size. My wife will be delighted." He grinned at Mr Thomas. "A word of warning. You're next in line for their gratitude, so brace yourself."

"Oh dear," Mr Thomas said mildly. "By the way, you've missed the news. Mr Belham has just told us we're to have a television crew here, making a film."

"He mentioned it this morning," Mr Seymour nodded. "But he didn't seem too keen."

"A possible explanation for his change of mind," Mr Thomas grinned, "is that the TV company are going to re-surface the school playground for one scene, and provide new gym mats for another. Ours are too tatty. They'll present them to the school when they've finished."

The next day a gang of workmen began to rip up and re-lay the asphalt playground, while carpenters and electricians swarmed in and around the gymnasium. Then rumour after rumour after rumour swept through the school.

Mr Belham called all the classes to the assembly hall and explained that the well-known children's programme presenter, Charlie Radburn, would be filming some scenes for his series, *Chuckles with Children*.

He let the excited babble of voices die down, then told them that as only the gymnasium and playground would be used by the TV company, there would be no interference with normal lessons. After warning them not to get in the workmen's way, he dismissed them.

The asphalters finished after only two days and everyone examined the new surface, then lost interest.

Someone in 2D produced a ball and a kickabout started. The old playground had been pitted with potholes, both shallow and deep. A high lob at the heap of coats that represented the goal, often hit the edge of a pothole and bounced back the way it had come. An attempted pass would bounce away at all angles. The lads were enchanted with the new smooth surface, but Nellie and the handful of girls who often joined in, were not impressed. Having a feminine delight in the unexpected, they found the new surface boring.

The banging and thumping in the gymnasium

aroused everyone's curiosity. Then a senior pupil was sent over on an errand and he reported that they had built a classroom in the gym with desks twice the normal size. The information spread around the school, and some disbelievers attempted to see for themselves, but were repelled by the workmen.

Early the following day all noises from the gym ceased and assorted sized vans drove into the school grounds, some pulling caravans, and cameras were set up. Electric cables snaked around the edge of the playground, and at break, Charlie Radburn arrived in his Rolls.

The whole school was assembled and even the teachers missed their cups of tea to watch. When he alighted from the car, hundreds of pairs of eyes examined him intently.

He was elegantly suited, and his rather overlong wavy blonde hair was immaculate. While his figure was slim and youthful, the more observant of the spectators noticed that he looked a lot older than he appeared on television.

Ignoring his audience, he examined the playground surface, spoke to a few technicians, and was ushered into the gym.

Just before the bell went for the end of break, a coach drove in and disgorged a cheerful and somewhat untidy crowd of extras who conversed at the tops of their voices, and when waved at, waved back and shouted, "Hello, darlings." The whole school was enchanted with them, and the teachers had a difficult time getting everyone mustered to return to their classrooms.

At noon, school dinners were bolted and pupils rushed into the playground. The cameras were set up and to everyone's delight the actors were dressed in old-style shorts and blazers and wore school caps. The actresses were in gymslips.

They clustered around the director, who was giving them their instructions, while workmen tipped and levelled a couple of barrowloads of soft soil, just off the asphalt, and wet it with buckets of water.

Charlie Radburn emerged from his caravan and all the actors went on to the pitch, one of them carrying a football. They formed sides and faced each other, then Charlie Radburn came on doing his famous schoolboy walk. A camera tracked behind him as he went to the centre forward position and the ball was placed at his feet.

"Ready, everyone?" the director called. He slapped his hands together. "Action."

Charlie Radburn tapped the ball and moved slowly up the playground with the camera following. The other players made fake interceptions. After a few yards the director shouted, "Stop." Everyone froze and, as Charlie Radburn walked off the pitch, an actor resembling him very closely walked on and took up the recently vacated position. On the director's signal, he began to swerve up the pitch with the ball, and the actresses in the gymslips jumped up and down squealing and clapping their hands. Someone tripped him and as he fell a number of players flung themselves upon him.

The director shouted "Stop."

The players on top of the unfortunate double got up and helped him to his feet.

Charlie Radburn came over and placed himself carefully on the ground and the group lowered themselves gently on to him and the filming started again.

The ball was kicked past the group on the floor and they clambered to their feet and chased after it.

The camera stayed on Charlie Radburn, he shook his head and stood, pretending to be dazed. Then he rolled around doing his famous staggering walk.

After a few minutes, the director stopped the action and Charlie Radburn's double came on again. The game started and the double raced up the edge of the asphalt, where the soil had been soaked with water. As he came to it, the others piled on him again, flattening him into the glutinous mess.

Then they got up and moved away. The camera tracked over to where the double was spreadeagled in the mud. He lay there for a few moments more, then climbed slowly to his feet, turning to face the camera.

There was no need for the star to come on, plastered from head to foot in mud, the double was unrecognisable. Only the whites of his eyes showed. The camera moved in for a close-up of his face and the director shouted, "Cut."

Eventually the actors went inside the gym for the classroom scenes and the playground was at the disposal of the pupils again. 2D had lost interest in Charlie Radburn, mostly on the grounds that he wasn't very funny, and the treatment of his double was inhumane.

* * *

At break the following day, 2D were having a kickabout while most of the senior pupils hung around the gym trying to see what was going on, when the Press arrived.

Photographs were taken of the filming of the classroom scenes, and afterwards they went outside and Charlie Radburn posed with the other actors. Then he posed by himself, pretending to fire a catapult, sucking a lollipop, peering around a corner.

One of the photographers noticed 2D playing football and asked Charlie Radburn if he would pretend to referee the match. Knowing the value of publicity, he agreed and went into the gym to borrow a whistle from the props man.

After snarling at him because there was a little delay in finding one, he shouldered his way through a group of extras and emerged with the whistle and his professional friendly smile. 2D eyed the approaching group warily.

"Now we'd all like out photographs taken, wouldn't we?" Charlie Radburn beamed. "We can show them to our friends." He took their silence for assent and, slapping his hands, he asked them to line up for a kick-off. Then he noticed Nellie and a couple of other girls.

"Who are they?" he asked.

Johnno stepped forward and pointed to Nellie. "She's a striker and the others —"

"No, no, no," Charlie Radburn protested, his smile becoming wider and little more fixed. "I mean, girls do not play football, at least they didn't when I was a little boy."

"They do now," Nellie said coldly. "There's a girls'

football league, and what about Dick Kerr's girls? My mam played for them."

The other girls began citing examples.

Miss Lomax, who was on playground duty, came forward. "Come on, girls," she said. "Just while they take the photos."

"All right, miss," Nellie said reluctantly.

The Englishmistress put comforting arms around Nellie and Joan and led them away.

Mr Belham gazed out of his study window feeling at peace with the world. Mr Croft had somehow stubbed his toes and would be off for the duration of the filming, and most of 2D were playing football, well away from the gym where the rest of the pupils congregated to watch the filming. He was about to turn away when he saw Charlie Radburn leave the gym accompanied by photographers and make for 2D, the rest of the school milling behind.

A feeling of foreboding swept over the headmaster, and he left his study and hurried from the school towards the playground.

2D lined up reluctantly, and when Charlie Radburn blew his whistle, began to play half-heartedly. Brain passed the ball to Johnno, but before Johnno could intercept it, Charlie Radburn gave it an awkward kick and it spun off the pitch.

"I thought he was supposed to be a blooming referee," Big Davo said indignantly.

The ball rolled towards where Miss Lomax and the girls stood. "Pass the ball over here, little girl," Charlie

Radburn called. Then he winked at the boys. "If you can kick it that far."

Nellie stepped forward, her face grim, and neatly trapped the ball. Then, as she stepped back a few paces, Mr Belham pushed through the spectators and picked it up.

"All right, Nellie," he said rather breathlessly, "I'll do it."

Cameras clicked and Charlie Radburn spun to face them. Behind him the headmaster clutched the ball to his chest, and realised he was too far away to throw it, and that most of the school was watching him.

He took a deep breath, bounced it and aimed a wild kick. Fortune favoured him, his left foot connected with the ball just right. It whizzed across the playground and hit Charlie Radburn on the back of the neck. The whistle shot out of his mouth and his long wavy blonde hair sailed up and landed on the Ant's shoulder. He fell clutching at Big Davo and Johnno.

Everyone milled around shouting confusedly.

The Ant, bewildered by all the sudden activity, noticed the wig. Convinced he was being attacked by a largish animal of hairy persuasion, he flung it to the ground and began to stamp on it.

In the teachers' room the day after the TV people had left Mr Belham read out a letter thanking them for their co-operation, and promising to let them know when the scenes filmed would be shown.

"It's very nice of them," Miss Lomax said when he had finished.

"It was," the headmaster agreed. "I must confess I was rather worried when they asked if they could film here, but everything went well."

The room became quiet and one of the younger teachers sniggered.

"Well, almost everything," Mr Belham blushed.

"It was a hell of a kick," Mr Thomas consoled him.

"The camera crew passed the same remark," Mr Belham said, fighting to keep the pride out of his voice. "And the props man insisted on shaking my hand."

"I'll bet that's one scene they won't be showing," Mr Seymour grinned.

"It'll take a while for everyone to settle down again," Miss Lomax sighed.

"It may take longer." The headmaster was full of gloom. "I glanced out of my study window earlier on and saw Davis, Johnstone and Hopkins miming the incident. It appeared to occasion great amusement."

"All things pass," Mr Gamboge remarked, as he drifted past towards the teapot.

As things turned out, Mr Gamboge was right. No one had taken into consideration the start of a new football season. The filming was forgotten and the relative merits of footballers and teams were discussed, sometimes heatedly. Occasionally punches were exchanged. As this was normal for the time of year, it helped everyone to slip into routine again. 2D's first lesson was history and Mr Seymour was taking them through the Kings and Queens of England.

As 2D had no interest at all in the Kings and Queens of England, it was heavy going. He knew that

2D liked the smaller details of history, so sometimes he would tell them what it would be like to be a twelve year old in different periods of history.

They liked to know how an ordinary bowman at Agincourt would live, or a young powdermonkey on one of Nelson's ships. In this way he hoped they would remember larger events by association. The lesson went normally enough until Mr Seymour reached Henry the Eighth, and Nellie Allbright developed a dislike of the Monarch because of the way he treated his wives.

Her lips thinned as she heard of Ann Boleyn's fate. The mention of Jane Seymour prompted her to ask if she was any relation. She listened in stony silence to the fate of the others.

"He wouldn't have chopped my head off, sir, if I'd been one of his wives," she told Mr Seymour. "I'd have stuck a knife in him."

The other girls, their attention aroused by Nellie's indignation, applied their minds to alternative methods of disposing of the King.

"Poison is favourite," one of the girls claimed. "You could put it in his food when you were cooking his dinner."

"His wives were Queens," Big Davo butted in. "They wouldn't be cooking his dinner. Anyway they had food tasters, so it wouldn't work."

"You could slip the poison in his beer," Joan Alison suggested. "I'll bet he wouldn't let anyone taste that first."

"A small barrel of gunpowder would do it," the

Ant declared. "Wait until he's asleep, bung it under his bed and light the fuse."

"That's clever," Nellie snapped. "The Queen staggering upstairs with a barrel of gunpowder on her shoulder and nobody notices."

"She's right, Ant," Brain grinned. "Quasimodo might get away with it, but not one of Henry's wives."

Mr Seymour glanced at his watch. The lesson was nearly over, so he let the class determine the best method of assassination. He reasoned that it would help some facts about Henry to stick in their minds. At least Nellie would remember Jane Seymour when the exams came up.

The bell went and Mr Seymour dismissed the class. They left still throwing fresh ideas at each other. Nellie and Joan went off with the girls, still indignant at Henry's lifestyle.

Brain stopped Big Davo and the others in the corridor that led to the teachers' room.

"What's up?" Johnno asked.

"We still haven't squared Mr Thomas for giving us that lift," Brain said sternly.

"We don't know what he'd like," the Ant pointed out.

"That's why we're here," Brain said. "We'll ask him."

A little time later, they were in the playground feeling quite pleased with themselves.

"That didn't take long," Brain said with some satisfaction.

Moving to a quiet corner, Big Davo pulled a

battered tennis ball from his pocket, dropped it, trapped it with his foot and tapped it to the Ant. "Thanks to Johnno," the Ant said, passing it to Brain.

They all looked at Johnno proudly and he blushed.

Nellie and Joan came over to join them, having exhausted the subject of Henry the Eighth.

The Ant saw them first. "I hope you're not going to go on about that Henry business," he said sternly.

Nellie waved a hand, dismissively. "Him? He's not worth bothering about. Anyway he's dead."

"You got him, did you?" Big Davo sniggered.

Nellie ignored him. "It just popped into my mind that we haven't paid Mr Thomas back for that lift. I think we.should do something."

The boys grinned at each other triumphantly.

"We've seen him," the Ant bragged. "And it's fixed."

The girls looked at them open mouthed.

"Tell us," Joan pleaded, recovering first.

"Well," said Big Davo, appointing himself spokesman. "He said he didn't want anything at first, but we pushed him and he said that he'd always wanted a book of amazing facts, like the one Johnno has."

"And you said you'd give it to him?" Nellie asked Johnno.

Johnno nodded and tried to look modest.

Joan looked at him admiringly. "Well, I think it was very nice of you."

All the admiration focused upon him unsettled Johnno and he felt an urgent desire to tell the truth. "I was fed up with the blooming book anyway," he blurted.

The others looked at him in amazement.

"You were?" Brain queried.

Johnno nodded. "It says at the start of the book that you will amaze and delight everyone with your knowledge."

"Some of the facts were interesting," Big Davo consoled him, but his voice lacked conviction.

"And a lot ot them weren't," the Ant grinned.

"Shut up," Nellie told him. Then she turned to Johnno. "Go on."

"Well, some people weren't amazed and delighted," Johnno went on bitterly. "I've never had so many people wanting to belt me one in my life before. Then what happened with my dad last Sunday was the last straw."

He had their attention now. "Go on," Joan and Nellie urged together.

"Well," Johnno went on. "Every Sunday my dad has a kip on the sofa after his dinner. I was reading some amazing facts and it said, when someone is dreaming, his eyes can be seen moving under his eyelids. I thought I'd have a look and see if dad was dreaming. His head was in the shade and I couldn't see properly, so I got my torch and shone it in his face." He paused and shook his head at the memory.

"And?" Brain prompted.

Johnno shuddered. "My face was very close to his and then he opened his eyes. I didn't like the way he was looking at me, so I thought I'd better say something. The only thing I could think of was another amazing fact. I asked him if he knew that in South Bend, Indiana, in 1905, a chimpanzee was fined for smoking in public."

"What happened then?" Big Davo asked, trying not to laugh.

"He went berserk," Johnno said sombrely. "Good job my mam was handy, she probably saved my life. Dad told her that either him or me would end up in a lunatic asylum."

Nellie looked worried. "I hope people don't want to hit Mr Thomas when he starts telling them amazing facts."

"It's not very likely, Nellie," Brain soothed. "He's six feet two inches tall and weighs fifteen stones."

"Come on, girls," the Ant encouraged, tapping the ball towards them, "let's have a bit of a kickabout before the bell goes."

True to his word, Johnno arrived at school early the following day and intercepted Mr Thomas. "Here's that book, sir," he said handing it to the teacher. "It says inside that you will amaze and delight your friends with the facts inside, but you won't, sir. They'll just get ratty with you."

Mr Thomas gave him a friendly pat on the shoulder. "Thank you for the book and your warning, Johnstone. I promise to be careful."

"You're welcome, sir," Johnno blushed.

A few minutes later, Mr Thomas strode into the teachers' room and called for attention. "Ladies and gentlemen," he said. 'I have here Johnstone's legendary book of amazing and bizarre facts. I suggest we all read it in the hope that we may develop mental antibodies to the information within. I thank you."

He placed the book on the table, close to Mr Dickens who opened it and began to read. After a muttered "good heavens", a couple of other teachers began to read over his shoulder.

Mr Thomas poured himself a cup of tea and sat down. Miss Lomax looked at him admiringly. "You can be very articulate at times, Mr Thomas."

Mr Thomas inclined his head. "Thank you, Miss Lomax."

"How," Mr Seymour asked, "did you get hold of it?"

"A flash of genius," Mr Thomas said modestly. "They wanted to return the favour of the lift and I hinted heavily about the book."

"And Johnstone parted with it willingly?" Miss Lomax queried.

"He appeared to be glad to get rid of it," Mr Thomas assured her. "He also warned me of the dangers of imparting unwanted information."

"I hope you heed his warning," Mr Seymour said.

Then Mr Croft entered the room limping slightly. "Any chance of a cuppa?" he asked.

Mr Thomas reached for the teapot and poured him out a cup. "I heard that you had an accident," he said, passing him the cup.

Mr Croft nodded and sugared and milked his tea broodingly. "It was by the boilerhouse," he said. "I imagined it was a football in the long grass, but it was a big stone ball. I didn't find that out until I kicked it. I thought I'd broken all my toes."

"A stone ball," Miss Lomax said innocently. "How odd. I wonder how it got there?"

"I was wondering where it went," Mr Croft said bitterly. "It wasn't there when I went back to look for it. I remember thinking it looked like one of those stone balls you see on the gates of old houses."

Mr Thomas smothered a grin and glanced at Mr Seymour, who avoided his eyes. Then Mr Croft's attention was attracted by the group around the book.

"What's going on there?" he asked.

"They are reading a book of strange and bizarre facts," Miss Lomax answered.

"I like that kind of stuff," Mr Croft started limping towards the group, clutching his cup.

Mr Seymour watched him go up the room. "I have a load of hedge clippings and garden rubbish in my car trailer," he said. "I was going to ask Mr Croft to burn it in the school incinerator, but I feel responsible for his limp."

Mr Thomas said, "I'll ask him if you like."

At this point the headmaster came in. "I just want to remind you that the school inspectors will be coming this afternoon, so be on your toes." He consulted his clipboard. "I see that 2D have swimming this afternoon, so they will miss the chance to air their knowledge." Beaming happily, he left.

Mr Seymour picked up his briefcase. "You'll speak to Mr Croft?"

"Leave it to me," said Mr Thomas.

Mr Belham felt at peace with the world as he offered the inspectors tea and biscuits. Everything had gone well, right from the start of the afternoon, when he had stood at his study window and watched 2D march smartly out of the school escorted by Mr Thomas and Miss Lomax.

The inspection had gone well too, and Mrs Mottram, of the kitchen staff, had brought the tea tray in as soon as they had arrived back at his study.

The inspectors indicated that they would like tea, and just as Mr Belham was about to pour, Mr Croft passed the window clutching a large bundle of twigs. The path ran close to the window, and some of the twigs scratched at the glass.

The headmaster took a deep breath and began to pour. When the social chit-chat was out of the way, and they were sugaring their second cups of tea, the older inspector said casually, "I hear that there was some sort of incident involving Charlie Radburn when the TV people were filming here."

"Ah, yes," the headmaster admitted. He cleared his throat. He had told the story a couple of times since the incident and it was beginning to improve with the telling. As he drew breath to start, Mr Croft scratched his way past the window for the fourth time, carrying his biggest bundle of twigs yet.

"Who is that man?" the older inspector asked.

"Mr Croft, the school caretaker," Mr Belham replied. "I can't imagine what he's doing."

"Perhaps he's building a nest," the younger inspector grinned.

Mr Belham's eyes went wide, and his cup rattled on his saucer.

10

It was an unusually warm sunny day in October, but there was an air of gloom about the group that stared out of the top windows of the bus at the almost bare trees and the drifts of yellow leaves in the gutters.

"Next stop is ours," Nellie said as she and Joan picked up the plastic carrier bags containing the sandwiches and lemonade that would sustain the fishing expedition.

The group stood and watched the bus until it went out of sight around a curve in the road.

"This is probably the last time we'll get that bus until next year," Brain sighed.

Big Davo had a complaint of his own. "You can see through the bushes and trees. A couple of years ago it was like a jungle around here."

They trudged silently up the twisting lane that led to a hump-backed stone bridge and the canal. Johnno moved to the edge of the lane until he was ankle deep in a drift of dead leaves, and began to shuffle his feet.

"I like doing this," he said to Nellie and Joan.

"We know," Nellie said shortly.

Johnno glared at her. "How do you know?"

"Because you wouldn't do it if you didn't like doing it," Joan snapped. "No one's twisting your arm."

Irritated by this unanswerable feminine logic, Johnno stopped shuffling his feet in the leaves and strode off to catch up with the boys.

"That's it," Nellie snapped. "That is blinking it. Come on, Joan." She hefted her carrier bags and broke into a trot, followed by Joan. Nellie pushed past the boys and then halted, putting her carrier bags on the ground and her hands on her hips.

"Right, you lot," she snapped. "I've had enough." The boys stumbled to a halt and looked at her and Joan open-mouthed.

"Had enough of what?" Johnno queried.

"Enough of you crowd of misery guts," Nellie replied. "Every year summer ends. There's nothing you can do about it. Either you all cheer up, or me and Joan go home." She stood looking at them for a moment, then played her ace. "And we have the sangwidges."

Big Davo looked at them pathetically. "You wouldn't do that?"

"We would," Nellie and Joan said together.

"I'm not miserable," the Ant protested. "I've brought my new rod with me, the one I got when I won the painting competition, I'm dying to use it."

"Well," said Johnno shocked. "You said it was too good for the canal."

"I changed my mind," the Ant shrugged.

"Let's have a look at it, mate," Big Davo pleaded.

"We're not far from the canal now," the Ant said. "I'll show it to you then."

Big Davo, Johnno and the Ant quickened their pace and pulled ahead.

"Well, they've cheered up a little," Nellie said with some satisfaction.

Brain nodded, and eased his fishing basket into a more comfortable position.

Nellie fell into step beside him. "Would you do me a favour, Brain?"

Brain looked at her in surprise. "Sure, Nellie."

"I picked a camera as my prize in that competition," Nellie explained. "It's a smashing camera, but I've read the instructions that came with it and I can't understand them. I've got it with me, the man at the chemist put a film in."

Brain's face lit up. "Let's have a look, Nellie."

Nellie put down her carrier bags and fumbled in one of them. "My other camera has only two buttons, one for sunny and dull days and the other for taking the pictures." She pulled out a leather case and gave it to Brain.

He took the camera and gazed at it reverently.

"It's a beauty, Nellie," he said. "And it's as simple to use as your old camera, you don't even have to worry about the light, it adjusts itself. All you have to do is point it and press the button. If you're taking a photo of something more than ten feet away, just push this little lever over to the other side."

He handed the camera back, and Nellie took it hesitantly. Joan stepped between them. "What Nellie means is will you show her how to take good photos.

You've won competitions and had your photos on show at school."

Brain glanced at Nellie, who was looking at him hopefully.

"I'd love to, Nellie," he said. "We'll start with the pub at the bridge. I've often meant to photograph it, but I never got around to it."

Nellie hung the camera around her neck by its strap and picked up her bags. When they reached the bridge, the others were on the towpath to the right, helping the Ant unpack and assemble his rod.

"They'll be busy for a while," Brain said. "Come on." He began to scramble down the bank to the left of the bridge on the opposite side to the towpath. Nellie and Joan followed him, and they reached the bottom, breathless.

Brain slipped the strap of his fishing basket over his head.

"Leave the bags here," he said. "It'll be OK."

"We could have taken a photo from the bridge," Joan complained.

"If you did," Brian explained patiently, "all you would get would be a photo of a pub, nothing more."

He stopped and studied the pub on the other bank. "The canal bends here, Nellie. If you take a photo now you'll get the canal, the pub and the bridge all in the same snap. Do you see what I mean?"

Nellie's face lit up, and she lifted her camera.

"Don't forget the distance lever," Brain warned.

Nellie let the camera hang from her neck while she

wiped her hands on her skirt. Then taking a deep breath, she sighted the camera and took a photo.

"Try taking one kneeling down, Nellie, then one lying down," Brain suggested.

Nellie did so, and when she stood, Brain pointed to a bush. "Go past that bush and try and get a photo framed with leaves."

Nellie looked at him in surprise. "What for? I've got three photos of the pub and the bridge."

"Professional photographers will use a whole roll on the one subject, then pick out the best." Brain explained.

"Let's leave it at three until I get the hang of it," Nellie asked.

"OK," Brain laughed. "Come on."

On the bridge again, they looked over the parapet and saw Johnno, the Ant and Big Davo still admiring the Ant's rod, taking turns to cast an imaginary line with it.

"I'll ask them if they want their photos taken," Nellie said happily.

Brain shook his head. "If someone knows they are going to be photographed, they go all self-conscious. The best photos are those of people who didn't know they were being photographed."

"We sneak up on them?" Joan asked.

Brain nodded. "Instead of going on to the towpath, we'll go into the field then up through the bushes on the canal embankment. With a little luck they won't see us."

A few minutes later, they were trotting along the bottom of the embankment, and turning a bend they almost ran into a horrified Mr Gamboge, who sat with his brush poised to add another dab of autumn colour to his canvas.

They in turn stared at him in surprise. Nellie recovered first.

"Hello, sir," she whispered, not wanting to alert the others on the towpath above.

Mr Gamboge lifted his free hand and waggled his fingers in salute.

"We're in a hurry, sir," Nellie apologised. "Sorry we can't stop and chat."

"How sad," Mr Gamboge murmured.

They edged past the art teacher and began to climb up the embankment, turning for a final wave before disappearing into the bushes.

Mr Gamboge wiggled his fingers in return with a little more enthusiasm.

Nellie only managed to take one photo before she was spotted.

"What's the idea?" Big Davo asked.

"Nellie's trying out her new camera," Brain explained.

"What was I doing?" the Ant asked.

"Just standing there looking daft," Nellie giggled.

The Ant decided to ignore her. He handed Brain his rod. "What do you think?"

Brain tried a few imaginary casts. "It's a beauty," he said. "If I were you I'd try a few practice casts down the middle of the canal until you get the feel of it."

The Ant shook his head. "I'll be OK. You'll see."

"We'll try the sunken barge by the next bridge,"

Johnno said. "My grandad reckons there's been a pike there since he was a kid."

"I hope it's not far," Nellie said sternly. "Me and Joan have been humping these carrier bags since we got off the bus."

"It's just a couple more bends away, Nellie," Big Davo soothed.

They plodded along in silence for a while, then the next bridge came into view.

"Where's this sunken barge?" Nellie grunted.

Johnno pointed. "Just there, Nellie, where those concrete posts stick out of the water. My grandad said there used to be a place on the other bank where they stored grain during the war."

"Good," Nellie said. "I'll be able to put these blinking bags down. My arms feel like they're coming off."

"We've spare rods, Nellie," Big Davo said. "Do you want to try your luck?"

"No," said Nellie coldly. "I think it's cruel."

"*I* think it's daft," Joan added. "Fishing all day and then putting them back into the canal again."

Opposite the concrete posts, the boys moved back from the water and prepared themselves for a day's fishing.

Nellie and Joan moved into the thick bushes looking for a grassy patch to picnic. For a while, the only sounds were birds chirruping and the lap of water against the banks of the canal. Then came the sound of someone crashing through the bushes. Big Davo looked up from his rod. "What are those girls doing?"

"That's not the girls," Brain snapped.

They put their rods down, but before they could move, a well-dressed man stumbled through the bushes a few yards from where they stood. He looked wildly up and down the towpath, then turned and ran towards the nearby bridge, his breathing hoarse and exhausted. There was more crashing in the bushes and a policeman burst onto the bank and raced after him. The boys watched open-mouthed, until the two ran under the bridge and out of sight.

"He must have done something," the Ant said.

"No kidding?" Johnno was sarcastic. "We thought they were having a race."

Nellie came running through the bushes. "That man the Bobby was chasing," she gasped. "Joan saw him throw something into an elderberry, but we can't reach it. Come on." She turned and ran back the way she came, the boys on her heels.

Joan was standing beside a big bushy elderberry. "It's in there, see," she pointed. "But I can't reach it."

Big Davo pushed through the lower branches, stretched up, and eased a leather pouch out of its depths.

The others crowded around him when he came out with his prize.

He undid the lace at the neck of the pouch and opened it. Six heads came together as they peered in, then came six assorted gasps of amazement. Jewellery glittered in the sunshine.

"So that's why the Bobby was chasing him," Nellie gasped.

Big Davo pulled the lace tight again and tied it.

"Well, that's our day's fishing ruined," he muttered.

"How do you make that out?" the Ant snapped indignantly.

"We've got to find a Bobby and hand it in. Then they'll want to ask questions," Big Davo explained.

"We could hand it in on our way home," Nellie suggested.

Joan shook her head. "I don't think they'd be very pleased if we did that."

They made their way to the towpath and the fishing rods. The water in the canal glinted invitingly.

"There must be something else we can do," Johnno said desperately. "Let's have a good think."

Brain turned from picking up his rod and found everyone staring at him hopefully.

"Try, Brain," Joan coaxed.

Brain closed his eyes and scratched the back of his head. The others watched, hardly daring to breathe. Eventually he opened his eyes and said. "Of course." They gathered around him and waited.

"Mr Gamboge," he began. "Nellie, Joan and me met him by the other bridge, he's painting. I'll ask him to hand them in. He'll probably take them to a police station."

"Good old Brain," Johnno said proudly.

"We won't start fishing until you get back," Big Davo promised, handing Brain the pouch.

As Brain turned to go, Joan caught his elbow.

"Make sure he understands what you're saying," she pleaded. "When he's painting I sometimes think he's not with us."

"OK, Joan, leave it to me," Brain turned and began to trot towards the far bridge.

Constable Dukinfield was going off duty when the news of another big house robbery broke. This time a powerful car was discovered, broken down in a country lane. It was thought that the burglar was on foot in the locality. All available police were to be drafted to the area. The call came at an awkward time, because there was a needle football match on in Liverpool and all available personnel were on crowd control. The Superintendent of Constable Dukinfield's station spoke briefly to the policemen and women going off duty.

"We must all make sacrifices in the fight against crime," he told them sternly.

They watched with lacklustre eyes as he strode from the room. Then the station sergeant, a practical man, made an even shorter speech. "Think of the overtime," he exhorted.

They surged forward as one.

So it was that Constable Dukinfield found himself half sitting on the warm bonnet of a police car parked by the stone bridge adjacent to the *Bargee* pub. The driver, a young and rather inexperienced constable, leaned his elbows on the bridge parapet and gazed moodily down at the canal.

"What are we supposed to be looking for?"

"Anyone behaving suspiciously," Constable Dukinfield yawned. The young constable gazed around. "There's not a soul in sight, much less behaving suspiciously," he complained.

"Good," Constable Dukinfield folded his arms and settled himself more comfortably against the bonnet.

A stout man came out of the *Bargee* and shouted something. The young policeman looked at Constable Dukinfield enquiringly.

"It's the manager," Constable Dukinfield explained. "I'm on the committee of an angling club, and we hold our meetings here every month. He probably wants to ask me about the next one." He strode down the incline towards the pub. "I won't be long."

"He probably wants some advice about a pint of bitter," the young constable muttered cynically, leaning on the bridge parapet again.

After five mintues, two ducks waddled out of a field and flopped into the canal. As this was the highspot of his day so far, the young constable watched them intently until they vanished under the bridge. Then he ambled over to the other side to watch them emerge. He was about to lean out on the parapet when he noticed a figure trudging through the fields towards the bridge. He decided to abandon the ducks for a more interesting contact. The figure was carrying a large holdall, and tucked under his other arm was an easel, and he held a painting. The young constable strolled to the bottom of the bridge and waited until the figure stepped onto the road. "Good day, sir," he opened. "Beautiful weather for the time of year."

Mr Gamboge blinked in surprise. "Good day, officer. Yes, it really is pleasant. Have you noticed how the sunlight in late autumn has a light golden tinge to it, and the sunlight in full summer is a fiery yellow?"

"No, sir," said the young constable, "I can't say as I have."

"Have you ever wondered," Mr Gamboge went on with mounting enthusiasm, "what Van Gogh, used to the burning sun of southern France, would have made of our cool Autumn sunlight?"

"No, sir," the young constable said firmly. "I never have. Honest."

"Pity," Mr Gamboge murmured, losing interest and heading for his car, parked in the *Bargee* car park.

The young constable gazed after him. He felt he had made a grave mistake abandoning the ducks.

Mr Gamboge put his gear down carefully and shoved his hand into his jacket pocket for the car keys. His fingers met a strange object and he pulled it out. He stared at it for a moment, then his face lit up as he remembered. Webster had been waving it in his face. He had wanted him to take it to the police station. Overcome with curiosity, he opened it and peered inside. Little flecks of light danced and sparkled. He reached in with finger and thumb and pulled out a diamond necklace, holding it out at eye level he shook his head in amazement.

Then a powerful hand fell upon his shoulder and a voice said, "All right, Raffles, you're nicked."

* * *

Constable Dukinfield strode purposefully along the canal towpath.

"We had him cold," the young constable said in tones of disbelief as he paced beside him. "And you let him go."

"He's an art teacher," Constable Dukinfield said shortly. "I know where he lives, I know where he works."

"It could be a front," the young constable persisted. "He might be our man, Mr Big."

Constable Dukinfield gave a snort of amusement. "That man couldn't break into a Wendy House if you gave him a thermal lance. Keep your eyes peeled for the kids."

They rounded a bend and a group of children could be seen fishing. "That's them," Constable Dukinfield said, quickening his pace. Then the still waters of the canal, where the fishing party stood, seemed to erupt and a huge pike leapt into the air and smashed down into the water again.

"Blooming heck," Constable Dukinfield shouted breaking into a run.

"I've got him, I've got him," the Ant screamed, pulling back against a force that almost tore the rod out of his hands. He lifted the rod and it bent double.

"Lower your rod," Constable Dukinfield shouted, pounding up. "Sight along it, let him pull on the line." He glanced around. "One of you assemble the landing net."

Brain, Big Davo and Johnno collided as they made a rush for it together.

Constable Dukinfield turned back to the Ant. "Let him pull the line out for a few yards, then reel him in again. Keep doing it. Tire him. Don't let him out too far, though. If he gets in the reeds on the far side, you've lost him."

Nellie and Joan came rushing out of the bushes to see what all the excitement was about. Joan stayed to watch, but Nellie ran back for her camera.

The battle raged along the canal bank, with Constable Dukinfield offering advice and instruction and Big Davo keeping pace with the landing net. In the background, unseen by the others, Nellie took her photos.

Eventually, the pike tired and was reeled in and captured. They all stood on the canal edge and peered down at it as it thrashed about in the keep net.

"By heck," Constable Dukinfield said, slapping the Ant on the back. "It's a monster. Well done, lad."

They stood, grinning happily at each other, then the young policeman lifted the leather pouch and pointed to it wordlessly. Constable Dukinfield sighed and felt the weight of officialdom descend upon his shoulders.

11

When the hour went on for wintertime and the nights started early, children from the Duck Street area began to slip through the gaps in the rusted iron railings and gather on the barren square known to the council as "Greenpark Recreation Ground", and to the children as the "Rec".

In summer the ground was left for toddlers, who queued for a go on the swings, see-saws and round-abouts, under the watchful eyes of older sisters, and sparrows who liked dustbaths.

When the dark nights came it was, by unspoken agreement, the gathering place for the arranging of winter games. This didn't happen suddenly. The first few nights would be spent arguing about what to play and milling around aimlessly. Then they would settle in to winter routine.

This year, as usual, they were going through the arguing stage and Nellie listened with mounting impatience.

"I don't know why they bother with all this messing about," she said. "We always finish up playing the same old games. Someone should think up new ones."

"It isn't easy, Nellie," Brain protested. "Everyone knows the rules of the old ones."

Just then, two girls on the edge of the crowd screamed.

Everyone turned and saw a small figure with huge fangs distorting his face, holding out a cloak. Johnno stepped forward and peered through the gloom. "It's the Ant," he reported.

"Where did you get those teeth?" Big Davo asked.

"At the joke shop," the Ant replied removing them. "I look horrible, don't I?"

"You always did," Nellie giggled.

The Ant ignored her. "I'm one of the undead, like in that horror film on the telly last night."

Nellie inspected the Ant's cloak. "If your sister finds out you're wearing that, you'll be lucky to finish up undead."

It was then that Brain had the idea. "I know," he shouted. "Let's play vampires."

There was a silence, everyone looked at each other, then at the Ant, who had replaced his fangs.

"What's the rules?" someone from the crowd asked.

"I don't know yet," Brain admitted, "we can work them out as we go along."

"It'll be ages before we all get fangs from the joke shop," Johnno said, "so how will we know who are the vampires?"

"The ones being the vampires can tie their coats around their necks by the sleeves, they'll look like cloaks," Nellie suggested.

A boy from another school pushed he way through

the crowd. "Girl vampires don't wear cloaks like the fellers," he said. "They wear white things with a hood on, and they do what the man vampire says. He's the boss."

Those on the edge of the crowd stirred uneasily as Nellie advanced upon him.

"Girls are as good as boys, right?" She jabbed him with her forefinger as she spoke. "So girl vampires are as good as men vampires any day, right?"

Impressed by her logic and awed by her physical presence, the vampire expert agreed that this was very probably true.

The Ant removed his fangs to converse. "They chase after people like this." He stretched out his arms like a sleepwalker and made a growling noise.

"Girl vampires don't growl," the expert said, before he could stop himself.

Nellie looked at him thoughtfully. "What noise do they make?"

"They hiss, like this," the vampire expert gave a demonstration.

Nellie considered the two methods and decided that there was no discrimination in hissing, as opposed to growling. "OK," she said. "Us girls will hiss."

A place was decided on for the game. On the edge of a new shopping precinct not far from the park was a large cleared area intended as a site for an extension. It was stacked with builders' materials and no work had been done on it for weeks, because one of the tenants had refused to move.

On the way to the site, vampires were picked and

a few rules thrashed out. On arrival, Big Davo stood on a heap of sand and declared the far corner of the site where the lone house stood, out of bounds.

"You know what Mrs Toumby is like," Nellie said supporting him. There was a murmur of agreement. Mrs Toumby, a large rawboned widow, had been on television explaining her views. She had also attacked one group of officials with her umbrella and set her dog on another. Everyone was rather proud of her.

The first evening was spent in a tryout of the new game and a thrashing out of the rules. Before everyone went home, it was generally agreed that it had possibilities, and they all determined to invest in a set of plastic fangs.

"It's all right for the lads," Nellie confided to Joan. "You can make a cloak out of an old bit of curtain, but the things we wear will be tricky to make."

Joan had a flash of inspiration. "Needlework. We can have them made up in needlework class. All you need are old sheets."

"You're a genius, Joan," Nellie shouted. "Let's spread the word."

The next night a larger crowd than usual met in the "Rec" before going on to the site, and as there were more fangs and cloaks in evidence, the game was voted a success.

Each succeeding night drew more to the game and, despite the site being a large one, vampires and victims sometimes spilled out on to the well-lit road. As the area came within Constable Dukinfield's patch, it wasn't long before he became aware of the situation. There were reports from the occasional motorist, another from a local vagrant who appeared to be stone cold sober. As Constable Dukinfield had never seen him in this state before, it made an impression. Then the manager of a Bingo Hall, who ran early evening games for pensioners, complained that the place reeked of garlic.

Constable Dukinfield kept a quiet watch one night, and after a little thought, decided to do nothing. The only house in the immediate area was widow Toumby's and she and her dog were quite capable of looking after themselves. He made a point, however, of keeping the place under observation for a few minutes every night after he had checked the adjacent shopping precinct.

Unaware of Constable Dukinfield's observation, the game went from strength to strength. The Ant, who considered he had really originated the game, felt he did not stand out enough when most of the lads had fangs and makeshift cloaks. The following night he turned up in a papier mâché top hat, left over from a Christmas party, and once again he stood out. Then, inevitably, more top hats appeared and he racked his brains for another gimmick. At first it seemed insoluble, then going home one night he saw a workman fixing the gearchain of his bicycle.

The red glow of the rear light made his face look weird, and the Ant had his idea.

He collected all the coloured paper he could find, and in his bedroom he experimented with a torch in front of a mirror. A dark green paper made his face so hideous that he became nervous and turned on the light.

That evening he waited until the game had started

before making his way to the site. Creeping behind a stack of bricks, he hugged himself with anticipation as he waited for his eyes to become accustomed to the gloom. After a couple of minutes he heard footsteps coming along the pavement on the edge of the site. He crouched, ready, and when they neared he turned on his torch and leapt out growling.

Widow Toumby screamed and dropped the bottle of sherry she had won at Bingo. It hit a brick and shattered.

The Ant stared at her, terrified. The widow Toumby screamed again and brought her heavy umbrella down on the Ant's top hat. The torch dropped from his nerveless fingers and he turned and fled, with the widow Toumby pounding in pursuit.

When Constable Dukinfield had reported for duty that night, he had been introduced to a straggly-bearded young man in a duffel coat.

"He'll be with you tonight," the sergeant had told him. "He's studying sociology and it'll be some experience for him. The Superintendent's OK'd it."

Constable Dukinfield had no objections. He had shared his beat with a reporter once, and the shift had passed pleasantly, telling yarns and cracking jokes.

This shift was not very old when Constable Dukinfield realised that he and the budding sociologist were not on the same wavelength. The people that he and the reporter had called "villains", the young man described as society's victims. He droned on as Constable Dukinfield went about his duties enveloped in gloom. In the shopping precinct, the sociologist caught Constable Dukinfield's elbow.

"Just imagine," he said earnestly. "Only a few years ago they used to hang people in this country. Just imagine yourself watching me being hung."

Constable Dukinfield did, and cheered up considerably.

As they left the precinct, Constable Dukinfield became aware that the droning voice had stopped. He turned and saw the sociologist staring across at the building site opposite.

A lad had run out into the street followed by two shrouded girls with fangs. As he turned to face them, a cloaked figure jumped on him and the three dragged him screaming into the darkness.

Constable Dukinfield turned quickly away, tried the service door of a shop and found it secure. He could see the sociologist pointing, ashen-faced.

Then came the sound of running footsteps and the young man dropped his arm and ran behind him.

His face eerie in the neon light, the Ant pounded towards them. The impact of the blow had driven his top hat almost over his eyes, and his natural teeth had become embedded in the plastic fangs that now protruded at right angles to his face. To see where he was going he had to keep his head held right back and force his eyes to look down his nose. The overall effect was grotesque.

Behind him padded the implacable widow Toumby.

As the Ant shot by, Constable Dukinfield recognised

his pursuer, and he touched his helmet with his fore-finger in salute. "Mrs Toumby."

"I'm going to kill him," she confided as she passed, slashing wildly with her umbrella.

The Ant spun around a pillar box, cloak flying, and angled across the road towards the darkness and safety.

"I'm going to knock his head clean off his shoulders," Mrs Toumby screamed, leaking details of the *modus operandi*.

The two vanished into the gloom.

Constable Dukinfield stared after them. "Always the same on my patch. You no sooner get the werewolf season over, and the vampires start up."

"Aren't you going to do anything?" the sociologist whispered, peering over the policeman's shoulder.

Constable Dukinfield shook his head. "He was only a little one," he said indulgently.

Then whistling softly to himself, he continued his beat.

12

When the Vampire game was at the peak of its popu-
larity, the local council made Widow Toumby an offer
she couldn't refuse. Within days, she and her dog moved
to a house with a garden in a new area.

Builders came, and after demolishing her house,
began to fence the site off. Vampires and victims had a
few more days until the fencing was completed and a
watchman installed. The following night they were in
Greenpark Recreation Ground arguing for and against
other places to play the game. They had broken up into
small groups all talking at once.

"This is getting us nowhere," Nellie snapped.
"Every one is arguing and no one is listening." She
made her way in the gloom in the direction of a small
wooden roundabout, known as "The Wedding Cake",
intending to stand on it and call for attention. On the
way she stumbled over an object and almost fell. "Who
put that there?" she demanded indignantly.

Johnno peered down. "It's a tree trunk."

"I know what it is," Nellie said coldly, rubbing her
ankle. "How did it get there? There hasn't been a tree
in this park since Adam was a lad."

"Excuse us," said a voice somewhere in the region

of Big Davo's knees. A horde of younger children had appeared and they swarmed about the tree trunk like ants around a straw and carried it through one of the larger gaps in the railings with much grunting and irritable cries of "Lift your end."

The dispossessed Vampires and Vampiresses in the vicinity watched as they vanished into the night.

"Well of all the blinking cheek," Nellie began, then a voice from the crowd said. "They're collecting for bonfire night," and quiet fell upon the gathering.

"They're early," Big Davo protested. "It's ages yet."

"Three weeks," Brain said. "That's all."

"And if you don't start early all the best wood is gone," Johnno warned.

The gathering began to fragment. They were from different streets and different schools. Each group had its own traditional bonfire site, and there was a shifting and moving together. They may have been united as Vampires, but bonfire night was another matter.

In the uneasy silence that followed, the Ant had an idea. "When they pulled widow Toumby's house down, they left all the floorboards and joists in a big heap outside the compound."

Big Davo clamped a hand over the Ant's mouth, but the damage was done. There was a drifting towards gaps in the railings facing the old Vampire site, a drifting that became a stampede as the gaps were fought over and the more daring scrambled over the top of the park railings.

Soon the different groups were scuttling into the

darkness with as much old timber as they could carry or drag, unity forgotten as they moved warily past each other like strange dogs.

The crowd from Duck Street area did well, but once in their own territory another problem presented itself. Namely, where to store the wood. It should be in a private place and preferably hidden from casual observers. As bonfire night came nearer, anything combustible for miles around would be gathered and hidden.

Then raiding parties would go out looking for caches of timber belonging to other areas. This was a time of raids and counter-attacks. Everyone stayed out as late as possible, and slept uneasily. It was a time of friend against friend and street against street. It would end the day after bonfire night when the warring factions, now friends again, would wander around the various sites, estimating the size of bonfires by the still smouldering mounds of ashes, and swapping stories of the amount of fireworks expended while accepting offers of charred potatoes raked out with a stick.

In the staffroom one morning, the teachers were talking about the build-up to bonfire night. Mr Seymour had started the conversational ball rolling by remarking that already there were five bandaged hands in 2D.

"Four were caused by picking up used sparklers while they were still hot," he said taking a sip of his tea.

"I hate it the next day," Mr Gamboge complained. "The classroom smells of smouldering clothes. It's very unnerving. I always have a horrible feeling that someone is going to burst into flames."

The teachers were nodding sympathetically when Mr Belham bustled in, ushering before him a young man and woman.

"Good morning, everyone," Mr Belham said briskly. "Let me introduce Miss Earnshaw and Mr Waltham from the Youth Training Scheme. They have some rather interesting ideas they would like to discuss with you. I'm sure you can introduce yourselves."

Looking decidedly shifty, the headmaster glanced at his watch, tucked his clipboard more firmly under his arm and backed from the room smiling and nodding, first at the newcomers, then at the teachers.

They watched the door close behind him, then transferred their attention to the new arrivals.

The young man took off his duffel coat and flung it carelessly over the back of a chair, then he spun the chair around and straddled it, leaning his arms on the duffel coat.

"Before the introductions," he said. "I'll tell you why we're here. Get down to the nitty gritty so to speak."

He paused, collecting his thoughts and they examined him, from the woolly hat with the bobble on, down to his battered training shoes, taking in the baggy cardigan, roll neck pullover and tight jeans.

"We're in on a pilot scheme," he began. "We're going to organise just one huge bonfire in a safe area, and persuade all the local children to attend. If we can succeed, it will cut down fire damage and prevent the usual firework accidents." He wagged a finger at them. "But first we must identify with the children."

"Will the children want to identify with them?" Mr Thomas whispered to Miss Lomax. "The older pupils are pretty snappy dressers out of school hours."

"I would appreciate it if you didn't talk among yourselves, and listened to Mr Waltham," Miss Earnshaw snapped, her plump face indignant.

Miss Lomax's glance flickered over her, starting with the fuzzy ball of nondescript hair, oversized spectacles and the unfashionable long baggy dress. It rested briefly on the calf high button up bootees, and went back to the woollen shawl around her shoulders.

"Mr Thomas was admiring your dress," Miss Lomax said sweetly. "My grandmother had a shawl like that, I was livid when she gave it to the ragman. His name was Flint. You didn't know him, did you?"

"No," Miss Earnshaw hissed. "I didn't."

"Oh," Miss Lomax said indifferently, transferring her attention to Mr Waltham.

Only the women teachers and a couple of the older married male teachers recognised the brilliance of this cut and thrust and they gazed at Miss Lomax admiringly.

Mr Gamboge voiced an objection. "It will need more than two people to supervise an event of that nature."

"Ah," said Mr Waltham, "that's the beauty of this scheme. Once we are accepted, the children will accept others, there are a lot of us you know."

"My God," Mr Gamboge muttered, deeply shaken.

"We'll only be here at breaks and during the dinner hour to mingle and put our ideas over," Miss Earnshaw said. "We're meeting later with council officials to find a suitable site for the bonfire. We'll pop in to see the headmaster and give him a progress report. Doubtless he will keep you informed." Then the assembly bell rang and the teachers left the room with greater rapidity than usual.

True to their word, Miss Earnshaw and Mr Waltham could be seen wandering around, mostly with senior pupils at breaks and dinnertime. Word filtered through that the council had given permission for the bonfire to be built in Greenpark Recreation Ground, but the teachers noticed that the pupils did not seem wildly excited about the idea, although they gathered around the duo, who seemed willing to talk about any subject.

One afternoon, Mr Seymour was on playground duty when he saw Nellie, Joan and Johnno coming his way. They would stop at intervals and argue among themselves. Mr Seymour watched them with some curiosity and when they eventually neared, he said, "What seems to be the trouble?"

"Oh hello, sir," Nellie looked surprised. "We were looking for Brain."

"We wanted to ask him something," Joan added. Then her face lit up. "But you'd do, sir."

"I'm flattered," Mr Seymour said dryly. "Ask away."

Johnno jerked a thumb over his shoulder. "We heard those two telling the sixth formers that the British Army burnt Washington. Is that true, sir?"

"Quite true," Mr Seymour nodded.

Johnno looked impressed. "I knew we burnt Joan of Arc, but I didn't know about Washington."

"Not George Washington, Johnstone," Mr Seymour grinned. "Washington the city."

"Well, that wasn't nice, sir," Nellie was scandalised. "What did the Americans do?"

"They all headed for a place called Yorktown where the man in charge of the army, a gentleman named Cornwallis, was staying," Mr Seymour smiled down at their rapt faces.

"What happened then, sir?" Joan asked breathlessly.

Mr Seymour considered. "Well, they told Cornwallis to leave America with his army as soon as possible, and close the door quietly behind him."

"Did he, sir?" Johnno was fascinated.

"Oh yes," Mr Seymour said, "there were a lot of Americans and they all seemed very annoyed. Cornwallis might not have been much of a General, but he knew when he was being given good advice."

He waited as the three digested the information.

"That's amazing, sir," Nellie murmured eventually. "If anything else crops up, can we ask you?"

"That's what I'm here for, Nellie," Mr Seymour pointed out.

Nellie and Joan turned away, but Johnno hung back.

Mr Seymour looked at him enquiringly. Johnno made sure the girls were out of earshot, then he said,

"Brain's my mate, sir, but I think you're as smart as him, smarter even."

"Thank you, Johnstone," Mr Seymour inclined his head. "A delightful compliment."

"You're very welcome, sir," Johnno blushed.

As bonfire night got nearer, Miss Earnshaw and Mr Waltham did not seem to be having much luck in persuading the pupils to unite their efforts and have one big bonfire. Old traditions die hard. Teachers on playground duty noticed that the pupils were beginning to avoid the couple as their novelty value wore off.

There occurred two events that made the Duck Street pupils reconsider. One of the boys who lived in a house with a largish garden, and had a father who was away at sea, allowed his mates to store a large amount of bonfire material in his back garden. This was spotted by a scout from a rival gang and a raid was mounted. The raiders were spotted, and in the brawl that followed the wood caught fire. When the firemen had extinguished the flames, a toolshed had been destroyed and the plastic gutters on the back of the house had melted. Parents in the area, made wise by the event, examined their own gardens and yards and issued an ultimatum: Move it.

Then the local paper printed a news item about the scheme, and a picture of a young lady wearing a false beard and a bathing costume, posing with a giant rocket donated by a chain store. Around her feet were boxes of ordinary fireworks, a gift from the paper. The rocket was as tall as the girl and with it was a latticed metal tube that was to be used for launching it. There was great speculation in the school on the height the rocket would reach before exploding, and even the teachers admitted to being at a loss.

To the delight of Miss Earnshaw and Mr Waltham, the children's interest snowballed and a great mound of wood appeared in the recreation ground.

Miss Earnshaw pleaded with the council for old tarpaulins to keep the wood dry until the night, and an official came down to assess the job. He looked thoughtfully at the great mound of timber that was growing daily, and went away. Shortly afterwards a team of workmen arrived and removed the wooden wedding cake roundabout, the six scater rocking horse and the see-saws, on the grounds of annual maintenance. A few large tarpaulin sheets were dropped off, and the workmen left.

On the day of bonfire night, everyone in the vicinity of Duck Street was planning the evening. The pupils were determined to make it the biggest bonfire ever, and Miss Earnshaw and Mr Waltham spent the day assuring everyone that the rockets and fireworks would arrive on time. The teachers were surprised when a reporter from the local paper dropped in and asked if any of them would visit Greenpark Recreation Ground that night and give their opinions of supervised bonfires. They would, he explained, be guests of the paper.

Most of the younger teachers were going to a Guy Fawkes Night Dance, but Mr Seymour, Mr Gamboge and Mr Dickens offered their services.

After school Miss Earnshaw's and Mr Waltham's

reinforcements arrived, and the pupils rushed home for a hurried meal. Within an hour, the park swarmed with children and the bonfire grew rapidly.

Across from Greenpark Recreation Ground, Mr Clintock of Clintock Builders Ltd, had called for volunteers to assist the watchman for the night. Mr Clintock stood at the gate of his compound and watched morosely at the frenetic build-up of activity. A group of workmen joined him. "They seem to be enjoying themselves," one said brightly.

Mr Clintock, an admirer of King Herod, did not answer him.

"Get in the van, lads," he said. "A quick meal at the café, then back here before they light that bonfire."

As the men moved towards the van, the watchman with a big Alsatian on a lead, joined them.

"Shut the gate," Mr Clintock instructed him. "And don't open it until we get back." He looked at the dog, who was panting heavily and shivering. "What's wrong with him?"

"It's all the fireworks going off," the watchman explained. "It's making him nervous."

Mr Clintock sucked in a deep exasperated breath and strode off after his men.

The watchman moved a little further out of the compound and watched the activity in the recreation ground for a few minutes, then as he turned to close the gates, some bangers went off in the distance and a rocket soared overhead bursting into coloured flares.

The dog gave a yelp of fear, and leaping forward, pulled the lead out of his hand.

"Shane," the watchman shouted, but the dog raced from the darkened compound area across the road to the shopping precinct, and vanished down the service subway. Muttering to himself, the watchman set off in pursuit.

In the recreation ground, the frenetic activity had slowed. The bonfire stood magnificently high. All the larger timbers had been stacked by the senior pupils, and then they had gathered to watch the men assemble the launching ramp for the giant rocket, and the frames for the ordinary rockets and fireworks. The smaller fry still scurried around in the gloom picking up the still plentiful supply of smaller pieces and throwing them on the heap. Then even this petered out, and they milled about aimlessly for a while.

Then an optimist in the crowd shouted, "I know, let's spread out and look for more wood."

"There isn't any," someone answered scornfully. "We've collected it all."

"There could have been some dumped since we last looked," said the optimist moving toward a gap in the railings. A couple of his mates followed him, and them from lack of anything else to do, the rest began to follow.

"This is a blinking waste of time," Johnno complained as they searched around the edge of the Clintock Builders' compound.

"They've left the gates open," Nellie said.

They moved cautiously forward listening for any sound. Big Davo took a couple of wary steps inside. The other watched him anxiously.

"Be careful," Brain whispered. "or you'll find yourself wearing an Alsatian leg warmer."

Big Davo picked up a piece of brick. "Get ready to leg it," he whispered back. He threw the brick across the compound. It rattled and crashed in the darkness before hitting something metallic. Then there was silence again. After a pause they moved in to join Big Davo.

"Look at that," the Ant pointed. Broken planks and pallet boards were stacked in a corner. "They won't want them, they're smashed."

There was a moment's hesitation. Then Johnno said, "We'd be doing them a favour really."

They looked at Brain who was tempted and fell, "Well, I can't see any harm in taking the broken ones," he admitted.

Nellie grabbed one end of a splintered plank and Joan the other. Brain and the Ant picked up another broken plank, and Big Davo and Johnno staggered out with a pallet board. They moved across to the recreation ground with many a nervous glance behind them. Other marauding groups saw them and followed their example. Then when all the damaged material had been removed, a bonfire night madness seized everyone. Anything burnable was picked up and carried over to the bonfire.

Miss Earnshaw and Mr Waltham and their helpers were busy with the fireworks, a safe distance from the bonfire itself, watched by the senior pupils, so that the fresh fuel was added unobserved.

A few latecomers were grunting out of the compound with heavy scaffolding squares, when Mr Clintock arrived back with his men. The headlights of the van caught them and they heard Mr Clintock scream with rage over the clatter of the engine. They dropped the squares and ran towards the sanctuary of the recreation ground. The van squealed to a stop. Mr Clintock turned to his foreman, who sat beside him in the van. "Charlie, get those squares back into the compound, and shut the gates. If you bump into the watchman, don't touch him, he's mine."

The foreman leapt out of the van and Mr Clintock gunned the vehicle onto the road and raced from the main gates that had been left open by a thoughtful council.

"What's wrong, boss?" one of the workmen in the back of the van asked.

"What's wrong?" Mr Clintock snarled. "There's about eight hundred quid's worth of my planks and pallet boards on that stinking bonfire. We've got to get them off before they light it."

Then to his horror, a figure carrying a burning torch advanced towards it.

The crowd around the bonfire, alerted by the late-comers, watched the van anxiously as it raced towards the open gates.

Then Mr Waltham pranced up. "Shall we light the bonfire?" he shouted, waving the torch above his head.

"Yes," everyone screamed.

Mr Waltham was surprised and delighted at their enthusiastic response and he ran around the bonfire thrusting the torch into the brushwood on the inside. Fanned by a cold breeze, it crackled and spat, then caught. Flames began to move up the bonfire, becoming redder and hotter.

Then a van came roaring up and skidded to a halt a safe distance away. The driver jumped out in such a hurry he left the van door open and he ran to the back and flung open the rear doors. "Right, lads," he screamed. "Get my stuff off that blasted bonfire."

His men piled out and began pulling planks and pallet boards away from the crackling burning mound, and hurled them clear.

Mr Waltham threw his torch down and grabbed Mr Clintock. "Leave the bonfire alone," he shouted.

Mr Clintock, who was by now practically foaming at the mouth, grabbed Mr Waltham by the throat and began to shake him. His woolly hat with the bobble flew off and his longish hair flew this way and that.

Miss Earnshaw came screaming out of the gloom and, leaping on Mr Clintock's back, began to pound his head with her fists. Other members of the Youth Training Scheme came over, and, thinking they were witnessing vandalism, began to throw planks and pallet boards back onto the bonfire. Within seconds they found themselves slugging it out with Mr Clintock's men. The bonfire tilted, spilling burning cardboard boxes, clumps of hedge cuttings and lighter pieces of wood. These rolled amongst the combatants and were kicked out of the way.

Constable Dukinfield came through a side street into the Greenpark Recreation area in time to see Mr Clintock's van roar into the recreation ground, and had a premonition that all was not well. Quickening his pace, he followed it, and was on hand when Mr Clintock and Mr Waltham became locked in combat.

Grasping Mr Clintock's wrists, he pulled his hands from Mr Waltham's throat and snapped, "Calm yourself."

Mr Clintock gazed blankly at the policeman. "I was trying to choke him," he explained.

"I know, sir," Constable Dukinfield said. "We're trained to spot that sort of thing." He looked up at Miss Earnshaw, who was still beating a tattoo on the builder's head.

"Have a word with her," Mr Clintock pleaded.

Mr Waltham staggered across Constable Dukinfield's line of vision, clutching his throat and sucking in smoke-tainted lungsful of air.

"I think your friend needs help, miss," he said.

Miss Earnshaw dropped off the builder's back and ran to Mr Waltham.

"That was clever," Mr Clintock said admiringly.

Constable Dukinfield gazed around. The fighting had spread away from the bonfire. Figures struggled in the gloom, and the area seethed with children shouting advice and encouragement. Illuminated by the burning debris, two men struggled on the ground by the small rocket frame and as it tilted over, the fuses ignited. The more observant of the Duck Street pupils evacuated the immediate area.

Constable Dukinfield blew a blast on his whistle, and coincidentally the rockets screamed away. Everyone froze as they flashed overhead in a low trajectory. There were three salvos in all, each slightly lower than the last. When everybody straightened after watching them vanish into the night, Constable Dukinfield blew another blast on his whistle, but the sound was muted as the large box of fireworks went off. Roman Candles, Rip-Raps, Catharine Wheels and Flares banged, flashed and spun in all directions.

Children ran, cheered and shouted and the fighting went on. Constable Dukinfield dropped the whistle into his pocket and spoke briefly into his radio.

After a few convivial drinks with the reporter and his photographer, Mr Seymour, Mr Dickens and Mr Gamboge decided it was time to see how the supervised bonfire project was proceeding. As they neared Green-park Recreation Ground their taxi was passed by a police car, an ambulance and two large blue vans, known locally as "hurry up wagons". They arrived at the recreation ground as the police convoy drove in. By the light of the bonfire, they could see figures struggling together, children milling and shouting, and lots of small fires all over the area.

The doors of the "hurry up wagons" were opened and the policemen began to load them with great efficiency.

The photographer raced into the park clutching his camera, and the reporter followed at a more leisurely pace. The taxi driver and the three teachers got out of the vehicle and watched through the railings. Within minutes, the first "hurry up wagon" drove out of the park and turned past them. Trapped in its doors and trailing behind was a smouldering woollen shawl.

"She's leaving early," Mr Gamboge sniggered.

They were about to return to the warmth of the taxi when the giant rocket took off. Instead of going straight up, it roared into the sky in a high curving arc, siren device screaming, and in seconds had vanished into the darkness.

In the recreation ground, things had quietened down. With shoulders slumped, Mr Clintock was walking over to his van when the watchman squeezed through a gap in the railings and approaching the builder said, "I've lost my dog, boss."

Mr Clintock reached out with arms that shook with rage and grasped the watchman's throat. They were promptly picked up and deposited into the second "hurry up wagon".

The reporter came out of the park pulling his coat collar up, and joined the teachers in the taxi. "Back to the hotel," he said to the driver.

"What about the photographer?" Mr Seymour asked.

"He's in one of the police vans," the reporter grinned. "He got caught in the middle of a scuffle. Not to worry, they'll sort it out at the station."

The driver turned the taxi into a road facing the park gates.

"It's a bit further this way," he said over his shoulder. "But there's a crowd starting to collect back there."

At the top of the road where it joined another, they saw a fire engine and a police van outside a pub.

"It's a good night for stories," the reporter sighed,

stopping the taxi. "I know that police sergeant over there."

When the reporter got out, the driver glanced happily at his meter, then switched on the radio and tuned it to a local station, tapping his fingers on the steering wheel in time to the music.

The teachers leaned back and watched the activity outside. Some firemen came out of the pub yard dragging a hosepipe and began to roll it up. A flurry of movement as a couple of gesticulating customers were hustled out of the pub and deposited in the police van. Then the reporter returned and got into the taxi. Everyone looked at him enquiringly.

"It seems," he said, "that the pub was hit by a battery of rockets. Some set the rubbish in the yard on fire, and one came in with a customer and exploded in the passageway between the snug and the bar. A dart player missed the board and impaled another customer. Beer was spilt and a fight started."

The driver eased the taxi past the fire engine. "Talking about rockets," he said, "there's just been a newsflash. The steeple of Saint Grisewold's on the Hill was hit by a giant rocket. It blew out the clockface. I'll bet it was that one we saw blast off from Greenpark Rec."

The teachers digested the information in a thoughtful silence. Then Mr Seymour said, "We must find out how far it is from Greenpark Rec to Saint Grisewold's."

"Why?" Mr Dickens asked.

"Because," Mr Seymour grinned. "Someone is bound to ask us tomorrow. . . "

You can see more school stories from
Magnet Books on the following pages:

DENIS MARRAY

The Duck Street Gang

Class 2D are a force to be reckoned with, as Mr Wordsworth, the student teacher at Duck Street School, soon discovers. Even more experienced teachers find that 2D's enthusiasm is a little hard to handle. Ordinary school events can quickly assume almost nightmare qualities when class 2D are involved: there was the school outing that became a riot, the extra-ordinary affair of the hand grenades, and their revolutionary new version of the school nativity play . . .

Runner-up for the Guardian Award.

MICHAEL A. PEARSON

Winners and Losers

Nobody at Swanswell would ever have dreamed that the day of the governors' visit would turn out to be such fun. But Swanswell kids are more than usually adept at getting into mischief and, of the whole of Swanswell Comprehensive, Ducker, Chico, Killer Maria, Bugs and Murphy and the rest of Class 3L are perhaps the most talented of all.

'Funny, sensitive, irreverent and superbly written, Mr Pearson's stories are a joy to read.'

THE FINANCIAL TIMES

GILLIAN CROSS

Save Our School

It's not the best school in the world, but it's
their school, and it's a lot better than the
place they'll have to go to if Bennett School is
knocked down. Clipper, Spag and Barny
want to make sure they stay at Bennett. With
their unusual talents they draw up an aston-
ishing plan of campaign to save the school.
But all their stunts seem to go wrong somehow, and it looks as if Bennett School will be
knocked down after all . . .

The Mintyglo Kid

'He's a monster from outer space disguised as
a small boy!' Spag's terrible cousin, Dreadful
Denzil, had arrived. There was nothing Spag
could do about it. The boy with five years'
supply of Mintyglo toothpaste, and plenty of
ideas about what to do with it, had come to
stay with his family. How will Spag survive
his terrible ordeal? Can anything be done
with Dreadful Denzil? Clipper, Spag and
Barny rack their brains . . .

SAM McBRATNEY

Jimmy Zest

Jimmy Zest may be the bane of his teacher's
life – but is he really the undiscovered brain
of the whole school? Jimmy's schemes leave
his friends open-mouthed (and sometimes
empty-pocketed) but Gowso, Penny Brown,
Knuckles, Shorty and Legweak are usually
on his side ... Whoever else would think of
the Egg-Box Wonder, after all, let alone
dream up the Strong Stomach Contest?

Zesty

10p a week to insure all your rulers, pens,
pencils, dinner tickets, break biscuits and
sweets. It seemed like a good idea. 10p a week
against loss, theft or criminal damage. It was
a *brilliant* idea. Mandy Taylor, Shorty,
Gowso, Knuckles and Legweak all thought
so. But Penny Brown had her own ideas
about any scheme run by the dreadful Jimmy
Zest. One – nobody would get anything back;
Zesty was too clever. Two ... IT WOULD
GO WRONG!

PHIL REDMOND

Grange Hill After Hours

When Grange Hill closes its gates at night, a whole series of family problems opens. Ziggy Greaves, the new arrival from Liverpool, who has been off sick because Imelda, the school witch, stuffed fibre glass down his back, goes missing. Laura tries to help Julia sort out her over-protective father, which only increases the tension between their respective parents; while Gonch, also having parent problems, has to try and break into the school – which can only have one result – disaster!

Grange Hill Graffiti

Gossip and rumour are running thick and fast at Grange Hill with everyone wondering if there is any truth in the graffiti on the school's new Speaking Wall. What is Fay's latest preoccupation? What is really going on between Ant Jones and Georgina? How will the evil Imelda react to this unwelcome in-fluence on one of her gang? Calley has her own ideas about how to spread what is heard on the grapevine, and Gonch looks set to expose Mr Griffiths' secret – he is not known as the Chameleon for nothing . . .

PHIL REDMOND

Grange Hill on the Run

Challenge and confrontation are prominent at Grange Hill as the end of term approaches. Everyone seems to be having a run-in with someone else as adversaries clash in the most unlikely situations. Ziggy is still trying to get his own back on Imelda; Ant and Mr Bronson collide head-on; Zammo causes widespread despair and Danny seems to be entering into his own one-horse race.

PHIL REDMOND
and DAVID ANGUS

Grange Hill Rebels

Hopes are raised at Grange Hill when Danny Kendall leaves for urgent hospital treatment. Perhaps he will return to school cleared of his previous anti-social behaviour? But things don't work out quite as his classmates had hoped. And what's more, it seems that Danny is not the only rebel at Grange Hill . . .

These and other Magnet Books are available
at your bookshop or newsagent. In case of difficulties,
orders may be sent to:

Magnet Books
Cash Sales Department
PO Box 11
Falmouth, Cornwall TR10 9EN

Please send cheque or postal order, no currency,
for purchase price quoted and allow the following
for postage and packing:

UK CUSTOMERS

Please allow 60p for the first book, plus 25p
for the second book and 15p for each additional book
ordered, to a maximum charge of £1.90.

BFPO & EIRE

Please allow 60p for the first book plus 25p
for the second book and 15p for the next 7
books, thereafter 9p per book.

OVERSEAS CUSTOMERS

Please allow £1.25 for the first book, 75p for the
second book and 28p for each subsequent
title ordered.

While every effort is made to keep prices low,
it is sometimes necessary to increase prices
at short notice. Magnet Books reserves the right
to show new retail prices on covers which many differ
from those previously advertised in the text
or elsewhere.